Mike

Rachel says
you like Thrillers

Hope you Like
this one.

Merry Christmas

Michael Connelly

THE
CALYPSO VIRUS

MICHAEL CURLEY

authorHOUSE®

AuthorHouse™
1663 Liberty Drive
Bloomington, IN 47403
www.authorhouse.com
Phone: 1 (800) 839-8640

Published by AuthorHouse 11/13/2018

ISBN: 978-1-5462-6483-5 (sc)
ISBN: 978-1-5462-6481-1 (hc)
ISBN: 978-1-5462-6482-8 (e)

Library of Congress Control Number: 2018912443

Print information available on the last page.

Any people depicted in stock imagery provided by Getty Images are models,
and such images are being used for illustrative purposes only.
Certain stock imagery © Getty Images.

This book is printed on acid-free paper.

CONTENTS

CHAPTER 1

PAYBACK

By 4pm the USS *Little Rock* (LCS-21) was almost 140 miles northeast of Port Louis, capital of the island nation of Mauritius in the Indian Ocean about 700 miles east of Madagascar. The *Little Rock* was heading at 12 knots for the U.S. Naval Base at Diego Garcia. She still had about 1,160 miles to go when a fight broke out in the galley among the cooks beginning to prepare the evening meal.

A few minutes later, LCDR John Samuel heard about it over the intercom. Samuel was the ship's executive officer and was officer of the watch as of 4pm. Samuel, pushed the button on the intercom to hail Chief Petty Officer Andy Maguire, the only Master-at-Arms on board, and at 6'5" – 260 lbs – Samuel thought, the ship's enforcer – not that they had ever really needed one. He told Maguire to check out, and take care of, the problem in the galley.

Ten minutes later Maguire and Ensign Peter Hartley appeared on the bridge. Their uniforms were spattered in blood.

"What the hell…." Was all Samuel could get out of his mouth before Hartley hit him in the face with a broken metal rod. Maguire grabbed Samuel's arms and pinned them behind his back while Hartley impaled Samuel with the broken end of the rod. Samuel coughed up a mass of blood and went limp in Maguire's arms. The helmsman standing next to Samuel was Petty Officer Third Class

Marie Ricchio, who stared wide-eyed and stunned at the scene in front of her. Maguire grabbed her arms and Hartley impaled her too.

"The Captain." Was all Maguire said as he and Ensign Hartley started for the Captain's cabin.

CMDR Paul Hale was Captain of the *Little Rock,* and was sleeping. He had been tired all day. Up at 4am to square the ship away for its 6am departure, he hadn't slept well because – he thought – of that damn third glass of wine.

The President of Mauritius had hosted the Captain and his officers at a reception the night before at Fort Adelaide on Citadel Hill in Port Louis, where all official functions were held. Hale didn't like receptions to begin with. Then there was that obnoxious Admiral from the 500-man Mauritian National Coast Guard. "Admiral!" Hale had thought. Hell, the entire Mauritian coast guard consisted of about 6 PT Boat-sized vessels. In the US Navy, that "admiral" would barely be a lieutenant. Hale had to listen politely while this idiot explained to him that his LCS – Littoral Combat Ship – was really just a mini version of a frigate. Then Hale had his second glass of wine.

After the "admiral" came the second obnoxious asshole – that Arab professor who taught at some German university. He was the one who caused glass #3 of wine.

What the hell was this Arab Professor doing there at the reception anyway? What was an Arab doing teaching Latin and Greek literature? In Germany? And, if he was really a Classics Professor, why did he have so many technical questions about the *Little Rock's* weapons systems? Hale wasn't a drinker, so that third glass of wine gave him a headache all day.

CMDR Hale did not hear Ensign Hartley open his cabin door. He opened his eyes to see Hartley's face inches from his own. Someone was pinning down both his hands and feet. Hartley was pushing a metal rod against Hale's throat. Hartley's face was the last thing Hale saw.

When Maguire felt the Captain's hands and feet go limp. He reached up and put his arm around Hartley's neck and with one quick jerk broke it. He left Hartley's body on top of the Captain's and went to tour the ship.

He counted seven dead officers and the bodies of 28 dead enlisted men. That was everybody. That was the entire crew. All dead but him. Then he walked to the edge of the fantail at the back of the ship. The *Little Rock* was still at cruising speed making 12 knots although there was no one at the controls.

Maguire looked into the water. He knew that the nearest land was over 150 miles away. But it didn't matter to him. He jumped into the Indian Ocean.

✻ ✻ ✻ ✻ ✻

As his plane taxied up to its gate at the Dubai Airport, Professor Mustafa al-Khalid switched on his phone, looked at the screen, and smiled broadly. The text message on the screen said: "Enjoy your flight to Munich." It was code. It meant that both drones had worked, especially the one that sent the electronic signal to the *Little Rock* activating the Calypso Virus. By now, Mustafa knew, the entire crew were dead.

As he rubbed the scar tissue along his hairline he remembered the evening when the U.S. Navy sent a drone with a Hellfire missile to his engagement party killing his fiancée and his whole family. "How perfect!" He thought.

Mustafa al-Khalid was very pleased with himself. He had paid for all of the research that went into the virus. He called it the Calypso Virus. *Kalupto* was the Greek verb to "hide" or "conceal". "Calypso" was the Greek nymph who kept Odysseus on her island for seven years "hiding" from him all means of escape. Mustafa called his virus the Calypso Virus because it had no detectable symptoms. Under normal circumstances the symptoms were all hidden. Only when a specific electronic signal hit the virus did its symptoms – hysteria and rage – appear.

Mustafa's other two toys had worked well too. First, the drone. Only four feet in size. It had overflown the *Little Rock* several times while it was in Port Louis – completely undetected because it was so small. During these overflights the drone copied an electronic signature of the *Little Rock* so it could easily recognize it hundreds of miles at sea.

And, Mustafa thought, the "Leech" had worked perfectly too. The

Leech was an undersea robot that affixed itself to the water intake on the underside of the *Little Rock's* hull and introduced the virus into the water that would be desalinated for the ship's crew to drink and bathe in. That is how the crew would be infected.

And so, with the crew infecting themselves with every drink of water or shower they took, and when the *Little Rock* was so far from any port that no help was possible, Mustafa's men had set the drone off in pursuit of the *Little Rock*. When it got there, his men sent the command to the drone for it to send the activating signal to the virus that had infected the entire crew. Within minutes they were fighting each other. Within half an hour, every single person on the *Little Rock* was dead.

CHAPTER 2

THE NAGAMATSU NO MIZU

The intercom squawked "Captain to the bridge" just as Shigeru Wakabayashi, captain of the oil tanker *Nagamatsu no Mizu*, turned off his electric razor.

He had slept well. The company's agents had done well in Mombasa. He had dropped off a shipment of Japanese electrical appliances and had picked up a cargo of tea bound for Perth, Australia. The bonus had been a consignment of Kenyan coffee destined for their homeland in Japan. The Japanese had a modest taste for the dark rich coffee that Kenya produced. Wakabayashi had been lucky that his agents found the shipment. That means that they wouldn't be empty from Perth back to Nagoya. There would be a modest bonus for Wakabayashi when he got back to Japan.

A few minutes later Wakabayashi appeared on the bridge. "What is the matter of such great importance that you would wake the captain of this vessel up?" He said to the second mate, who was standing watch at that time.

"I am sorry, Captain. I didn't know you were still sleeping. It is this American frigate off the starboard bow, sir. We have dipped our ensign, as we should have; but no response."

"What do you mean, no response?"

"Sir, the American should have dipped her ensign too. But she didn't."

"Are you so shocked to find that there are American captains dumb enough not to know the protocols of the sea?"

"It's not just that, sir. The helmsman and I both looked closely at the American. We couldn't see anyone. Look you can see for yourself." The second mate said handing binoculars to the captain. "Her bridge looks empty. No sign of anyone at the controls."

"Hnnf." Snorted the captain putting the binoculars down a moment later. "Do we have crew on this ship who can do semaphore flags?"

"Yes, sir. Of course, sir."

About ten minutes later one of the *Nagamatsu no Mizu's* crew appeared on the bridge with a set of semaphore flags in his hands. Bowing to the captain and the second mate, he addressed the second mate: "What do you want me to say to them, sir?"

"Say 'American warship, please respond.' That is all you need to say. Just keep repeating it until we get a response." The mate said looking sideways at the captain who was looking sideways back at him.

The crewman went outside on the bridge and started signaling. When five minutes had passed, he had sent the same signal 10 times with no response from the *USS Little Rock*.

He peered in at the captain and the mate with a quizzical look. The captain growled, "Sound the horn. Sound the horn three times and tell the sailor to keep signaling. Maybe the horn will get the Americans' attention."

In the next five minutes the mate sounded the horn three times – three different times – while the sailor continued to signal with his flags. No response from the American ship.

"What now?" The mate said to the captain.

"We make for Perth." The captain said.

"Sir….. respectfully….. I think we should check it out further."

"Why?"

"What if this is some kind or exercise or game that the Americans are playing to judge the reaction of other ships when they encounter a warship with no signs of life? It wouldn't look good for us if we just walked away and then they reported us to the maritime authorities."

No it wouldn't. The captain thought to himself.

"And, what do you suggest?"

"Captain, I think we should lower a launch and go over and give the American a close inspection."

"And then what?"

"If still no response, then we should tell Diego Garcia."

"Tell them what?"

"That we have encountered that ship. Saluted her. Tried to contact her by radio and by signal flag. We have sounded our horn multiple times. But no response at all. So we sent a detail to inspect which found no one present on the bridge and no other signs of life on the vessel."

The captain thought for a moment. He didn't like deviating one minute from his self-imposed schedule. But, he thought further, if the mate is right; then we need to contact the Americans and let them know what we tried to do. And, after all, it would only take ten more minutes or so to send an inspection party."

"All right. Launch an inspection party." The captain said. "Let me know what they learn.

Thirty minutes later the captain was back in his cabin when the intercom squawked. "Captain, the inspection party is back."

"I'll be right there." The captain said into the intercom.

"Just as we thought, sir. The inspection party saw no one. No one at the helm. No one on the bridge. No one anywhere on the ship."

"All right. Send the Americans the message."

"Here, sir." The mate said, handing the captain a message form that read:

The "Nagamatsu no Mizu", freighter out of Nagoya, Japan, bearing 99 degrees at 6 degrees south latitude, 61 degrees east longitude, encountering US warship, frigate class, bearing approximately 40 degrees at 12 knots. No response from ensign salute. No response from radio inquiry. No response to semaphore. Close visual inspection revealed no personnel at the helm or on bridge. No personnel visible anywhere on ship. This message informational only. Breaking off contact. Continuing to Perth.

"Send it." The captain said handing the paper back to the second mate.

CHAPTER 3

DR. NICOLA ANGELINI

Nicola was born in Ascona, a pretty little village just below Locarno sitting on the top of Lago Maggiore in the Italian-speaking Ticino Canton of Switzerland.

Nicola's father was a math teacher at Le Rosey, an exclusive and very expensive school in Gstaad. His mother worked in the headmaster's office. Because of his parents' positions, Nicola was able to attend the school. The other students came from wealthy families all over the world. Many of the royal families from the Persian Gulf sent their children there. The school was very clique-ish. The Latin-Americans kept to themselves. So did the Europeans and so did the Arab kids from the Gulf.

Everyone knew that Nicola's parents worked at the school. So, the other European kids assumed that his family had no money and that he, therefore, was not of their social class. Nicola didn't have a lot of friends.

One friend Nicola did have was a Muslim, not an Arab, but rather a Turk. His name was Mustafa al-Khalid and he was from Istanbul. Mustafa didn't have many friends either. His family had a lot of money. But they made their money brewing beer and selling it in Turkey. Alcohol is banned by the Islamic faith. So, the rich Gulf kids used this as an excuse to shun Mustafa.

Mustafa was a quiet nerd. After Nicola, his best friend was a teacher named Tom Falkner. Tom taught Latin and classical literature. The Greek language was not offered at Le Rosey, but Mustafa persuaded Tom to give him private tutoring. Mustafa loved the Greek influence on his country and he excelled at both Latin and Greek. That was great for Nicola, who didn't do well in Latin. Nicola got Mustafa to tutor him in Latin.

Science was Nicola's strong suit. His father even said that Nicola was the best science student in the school. Mustafa, on the other hand, was not a science guy. So, Mustafa got Nicola to tutor him in chemistry and physics.

Over their breaks, Nicola often invited Mustafa back to Ascona where they would play tennis on the red clay courts along the Lake. During the Summers, Mustafa invited Nicola to Istanbul. He even paid for the plane tickets. Mustafa loved to show Nicola the beautiful ruins and all of the great classical architecture. The two of them would go off together and travel the country by train. In the Winter, on breaks, the other kids would go on expensive trips to Paris or Rome. Mustafa and Nicola just stayed at school and went skiing in the nearby Alps.

During their senior year, Tom Falkner lined up a position as a classics professor at the Maximillian University in Munich. Mustafa decided to follow him and study classics there too.

Nicola went to an excellent science school with the unfortunate and preposterous acronym SUPSI. In Italian, it was the *Scuola Universitaria Professionale della Svizzera Italiana*. In English, the school's name was almost as unfortunate: the University of Applied Sciences and Arts of Italian Switzerland.

The two boys kept in touch. Nicola's school was in Lugano, close to his home in Ascona. Mustafa was just a few hours up the road in Munich. They often spent breaks together.

As the college years went on Nicola was growing concerned for his friend. Mustafa hung out with the Arab crowd at the University and was getting political. After graduation, Nicola decided to go to medical school in Zurich. Mustafa went back to Istanbul to study Islam.

They still stayed in touch. Nicola persuaded Mustafa to come to Ascona for a couple of weeks one Summer. And the following year,

Nicola went to visit Mustafa in Turkey. It was then that Mustafa introduced Nicola to his girlfriend, Jasmine. The following Spring Mustafa invited Nicola to come to Turkey for his engagement party. It was the week of Nicola's oral exams at medical school. He couldn't go.

After a couple weeks, Nicola tried to contact Mustafa. No response. This went on for almost a month. Nicola was getting very concerned about his friend. He finally reached Mustafa after eight weeks. It was then that he heard the horrific story.

The engagement party had been on Mustafa's family's 100+ foot yacht off the coast of Kusadasi in the Aegean Sea. The US Navy had attacked the yacht in the middle of the party. They fired a Hellfire missile at it from a Reaper drone. Jasmine and her whole family had been killed. So had Mustafa's parents and most of the other members of his family.

Mustafa explained that – unbeknownst to him – Jasmine's father, a highly respected Muslim clergyman, was the head of the Muslim Brotherhood. The Brotherhood sponsored terrorist groups who had plagued the Americans. Jasmine's father had invited several high-ranking members of the Brotherhood's council to the engagement party. U.S. Naval Intelligence had been listening. They couldn't pass up the chance to get so many of the Brotherhood's leadership with just one shot.

Mustafa himself survived but was maimed. He told Nicola that he would have to have months of plastic surgery.

Over the next year, the two talked occasionally but didn't visit each other. Nicola really didn't know what to say anymore. Finally, he heard from Mustafa that he was returning to Munich to study with his old friend, Falkner. Mustafa was going to get his Ph.D. in classical studies.

Nicola had always had a problem with what he called "the money thing". His parents had always gotten along fine with their modest salaries. But, beginning at Le Rosey, Nicola had always looked with big eyes at all of the cars, and the clothes, and the travel that his rich fellow students enjoyed.

While in medical school, Nicola had got a job working at an assisted living facility caring for the elderly. He liked this type of work. He liked these kindly old people. He got along with them very well. So, when it came time to choose which field of medicine he would practice in he chose gerontology – medicine for the aged.

After Nicola got his license he began working at a state clinic for the elderly. The pay for a young doctor was ok, but not great. Slowly, he developed a strategy for augmenting his income.

Most of his patients had mildly degenerative diseases and came to the clinic once a month for treatment. As he became friendly with many of his patients, he observed that some of them were quite wealthy. To a few of the wealthier ones, Nicola made a bold suggestion. He told them that he was working on experimental treatments for their diseases that looked very promising, but that the clinic would not allow any experimental treatments - only treatments approved by the Swiss national medical boards. "Too bad." Nicola commented to several of his patients. "I think these treatments could really help people like you." The ruse worked on several of them. They asked if Nicola would treat them privately, outside of the clinic. They offered to pay him.

Nicola's "experimental treatments" involved administering drugs that made his patients docile and malleable. Nicola told them that the drugs he was administering were from Canada and that they were very expensive. The more docile his patients became, the more money he asked them for. This system worked quite well until – after about two years - one of his patients died. Nicola was shattered and stunned. The man who died was a dear old soul, whom Nicola genuinely liked. The man lived alone. His body was not found until he missed an appointment at the clinic. The staff had tried to contact him and eventually asked the police to look for him. The police quizzed the man's neighbors who hadn't seen him for several days. They thought this was unusual. The old man loved to walk around the neighborhood. The weather had been pleasant for the last week or so. But no one had seen the man out walking. Finally, the police obtained an order from a magistrate allowing them to enter the old man's flat. There they found him. He had been dead for over a week.

The clinic was able to obtain a copy of the old man's autopsy. He had died of malnutrition. The coroner's report noted that there were modest levels of adrephine in his blood. Adrephine has the effect of reducing brain function. It was the drug Nicola had been giving him. Although the coroner drew no conclusions, Nicola knew that it was the adrephine that caused the man to quit eating. That's where the malnutrition came from. That's how the man died.

Nicola was so shaken that he ceased all his outside treatments. He just went on working at the clinic. But, every chance he got, he kept up his new habit of expensive foreign trips – all of the trips he had dreamed of at Le Rosey and in college, but couldn't afford.

This lasted for a little over a year, until Nicola ran out of money. Slowly, he started "experimental treatments" again on his wealthy patients.

After about a year and a half of his new "experimental practice", another of his patients died – a woman this time. This one didn't hit Nicola as hard as the death of the old man had. He hadn't developed a strong relationship with this particular patient.

Nicola sat himself down and thought about his future. The medical examiner would undoubtedly find adrephine in the woman's system. But, in the old man's case, he had made nothing of it. He apparently never suspected that the adrephine was the mechanism of death. So, the coroner probably wouldn't suspect anything this time either. So, Nicola didn't see any reason to stop with the "experimental treatments" for his wealthy patients.

And so Nicola continued for several months until one day as he was emerging from the home of one of his wealthiest patients, he was approached by two men who showed him identification from the Federal Office of Police. They said they wanted to speak to him about "possible irregularities" in his medical practice.

They took him to their offices. They interrogated him about treating his patients with adrephine. They also interrogated him about the large sums on money that he regularly received from the patients, which they knew all about. After several hours, they said he was free to go. But they told him to return the following day at 2pm.

Nicola arrived the next day at two. He was escorted into the chambers of one of the presiding magistrates.

"Dr. Angelini. You have been conducting unauthorized medical treatments on certain patients for more than four years. Two of your patients have died. The drug adrephine was associated with their deaths. In the case of every patient on whom you administered unauthorized treatments, you received many very large payments – far larger than could normally be associated with any kind of medical treatment. In addition, all of your other patients that we have talked to about you have also tested positive for adrephine.

"Dr. Angelini, I don't know exactly what you have been up to; but it looks very, very ugly.

"You know, we Swiss have a worldwide reputation for the high quality of our health care. If word of what you have done ever got out into the world; our reputation would be dashed – shattered.

"I am not sure we have enough evidence to convict you of the murder of your two patients. I am not even sure we have enough evidence to revoke your medical license. And, I certainly don't want any long, drawn out legal proceedings about either matter where the entire world can see our dirty laundry.

"So, I am going to make you an offer, Dr. Angelini – one that you dare not refuse. Sir, you are finished practicing medicine in this country. If you are caught treating one more patient, we will immediately begin license revocation proceedings against you – and damn if the world watches. Do you understand me – understand me fully – Dr. Angelini?

"Yes, Magistrate." Nicola said calmly. And then for some strange reason, he blurted out. "You are leaving me with my license but you are not permitting me to practice. If I can't practice, what can I do?"

The magistrate gave Nicola a withering look and said: "Dr. Angelini, you can either learn another trade, or you can leave Switzerland. And, if you know what's good for you, you will choose the latter."

Two weeks later, Nicola arrived at Mustafa's home in Munich with enough clothes for a very long stay.

CHAPTER 4

DIEGO GARCIA

"Oh, shit!" Said Lieutenant Mickey Grayson, looking at the message that Petty Officer 3rd Class Brenda Heinz just handed him. "It's the goddamn *Little Rock*!" Grayson was the Officer of the Deck at the Harbormaster's Office at the Diego Garcia Naval Base.

"You sure have a mouth on you." Brenda said staring at him.

"Try to be nice. Cut people a little slack and look what happens? Shit happens! That's what happens!" Grayson said to himself staring right at Brenda but not seeing her.

"Like I said." Said Brenda again. "The mouth."

"Listen, Brenda, can you get me the skinny on this Jap ship?"

"Will do." Brenda said before heading back to the comms center.

"Damn, what rotten luck!" Mickey said aloud still looking at the message. When Mickey had come on at midnight, he noted on the status board that the *Little Rock* had been sending in all her nav data as she was supposed to; but she hadn't called at 2000 with a voice confirmation.

He asked the duty officer whom he was relieving, who shrugged. "You wanna rattle the old lady's cage, go ahead. Missed call-in at 20 hundred hours. BFD."

The "old lady", whom the duty officer referred to was 35-year old Lieutenant Commander Katy Bullard, the Harbor Master of the Diego Garcia Naval Base in the middle – literally – of the Indian Ocean.

An hour later, at 0100, the *Little Rock* had not called in again as they should have at midnight. *Rattle the old lady's cage?* Mickey thought – at 1am? No way. The *Little Rock* guys were just goofing off. Probably a new guy at the comm. No sense burning him just for a missed call.

By 0500, the *Little Rock* had still not called in. She had missed three calls, including the 0400 call. Mickey had a bad feeling about this, but he was relatively new too; and the thought of waking up LCDR Bullard at 5am was a seriously unattractive option.

And then, at 20 after six in the morning, this goddamn message from this fucking Jap ship. Can't raise them. Nobody visible topside. WTF? I mean really, WTF? Mickey was not looking forward to breaking the news to Bullard; but this time he had to.

Mickey thought he had better do this in person, so there he was knocking on the door of LCDR Katy Bullard's cabin door.

"M'am, it's Lieutenant Grayson. We may have a problem with the *Little Rock*."

"A problem big enough to spoil my day that's just beginning at 0630?"

"I'm afraid so, M'am. It's the *Little Rock*. Her data's been coming in ok, but we haven't had voice contact with them since 1600."

"Let me see." Bullard said opening the door and revealing a seriously attractive, dark-haired, female officer in pajamas. "Sounds like I'm going to spend this glorious day writing Letters of Reprimand for the asshole watch officers on the *Little Rock* AND two smart-ass comms officers on this base who weren't clever enough to get on the case of the watch officers on the *Little Rock*."

Didn't think this would be easy. Mickey said to himself.

"M'am, it's a bit more complicated than that."

"Oh?"

"Well, M'am, this Japanese freighter en route from Mombasa to Perth came on to the *Little Rock*. They saluted her. They tried to contact her by radio. They signaled her with semaphores. No response. So they sent a launch to check her out. They saw no living soul. Nobody on the bridge. Nobody at the helm. No one anywhere to be seen on the entire ship. The Japs were so freaked out, they called us. They sent us this." Grayson said handing the message form to Katy.

When she finished, she handed it back to Grayson and said: "Well, I'll be damned, Lieutenant, what do you make of it?"

"I have no clue, M'am."

"Did you try to raise the *Little Rock* yourself, Grayson?"

"No, M'am. I thought to wait instructions from you before doing anything like that."

"Well, in that case, why don't you give me a few moments of peace to get my uniform on and I will come to the comms room and we will call the *Little Rock*."

"Yes, M'am." Mickey said as the commander shut the door in his face.

Looking in the mirror while dabbing a washcloth over her face, Katy thought to herself. *No. No Letters of Reprimand for my asshole lieutenants. Maybe reductions in grade. But definitely a Letter of Reprimand for their senior officer, Lieutenant Commander Katy Bullard. The Navy always goes for the top man first…..and hardest. A Letter of Reprimand would mean that she'd never be promoted again. Oh, well.* She thought. *I guess I'd better start thinking about a post-Navy career.*

❀ ❀ ❀ ❀ ❀

"All right, Lieutenant, dial up the *Little Rock*." LCDR Bullard said as she entered the comms room 20 minutes later."

"Aye, M'am. *USS Little Rock*, this is Diego Garcia base, come in, please." Mickey said looking at his watch. Thirty seconds later, he repeated the message. And then again, after another 30 seconds. And so on, through 10 attempts.

Finally, LCDR Bullard walked to the base intercom and pushed a button. "Chief Serkis here, sir, how can I assist you?" Came a voice.

"Chief, where's the base CO?"

"We just talked to him in his office a few minutes ago sir. May I ask whom I am speaking to, sir?" The Chief asked. Bullard didn't bother to respond. She just pushed the buttons for the CO's office.

"Chief Menendez here, sir, how may I assist you?" A voice said.

"This is the Harbor Master. I need to talk to the CO."

"Yes, M'am. One moment, M'am." The Chief said as he put Bullard on hold.

"Vasquez here." Said Captain Octavio Vasquez, Commanding

Officer of the Diego Garcia US Naval base. "What can I do for you, Commander?"

"Sir, we may have a problem with an incoming LCV, the *Little Rock*."

"Talk to me, Commander."

"May I come and talk in person, sir. It's a complicated situation and we have a signal from a Japanese tanker that makes it more complicated."

"I'm here, Commander. Get your ducks in order and lead them in."

Less than 5 minutes later in Vasquez' office.

"Well, sir, she's about 1,100 miles southwest of here, coming from a courtesy call in Mauritius. Her nav data have been coming in fine. But we haven't had voice contact with her since 1600 yesterday. My geniuses did not bother to check on the situation until I got to the comms room 15 minutes ago. We tried to contact her just now, sir. Nada. Absolutely nada." Ricker said hoping she had adequately covered her ass.

"So, she's on course to us. But she's dark. Is that it, Commander?"

"Yes, sir, but there's more, sir. We had a signal from a Japanese tanker who spotted the *Little Rock*." Katie handed the message to Vasquez. They saluted her and then tried several different ways of raising the *Little Rock* but nothing happened. No response at all. They even sent a launch to look the situation over. They saw no living person on the *Little Rock*.

"This doesn't sound very good." Said Vasquez reading the Japanese signal. "As a matter of fact, it sounds very, very bad. What should we do, Commander?"

"Sir, I was thinking we should send an F-18 out there to check her out. An F-18 can slow down to a couple hundred miles an hour. Should be enough to get a good visual. See who's at the helm, who's on the bridge."

"Ok, Commander, but what if the Japanese are right? What if there's nobody to be seen. What then?"

"I don't know, sir. A ship with nobody aboard? How could that be? Where could the crew have gone? Could they all have died of something like food poisoning without calling in? It just doesn't make any sense at all."

"I don't know either, Commander, but it certainly doesn't sound good. Ok, tell Flight Ops I have approved the deployment of one F-18. They can call me if needs be. And, just in case, see if there's an "Arleigh Burke" anywhere in the *Little Rock's* neighborhood. There might be one doing piracy patrols off the east coast of Africa. If the F-18 pilot doesn't see anyone – like the Japs – we'll have to send a boarding party."

"Aye, sir." Katy said and then left.

Vasquez had always gone by the book. But this situation with the *Little Rock* wasn't in the book, he told himself. The Chief of Naval Operations had the reputation of being a hands-on, no bullshit officer. Vasquez thought about what he might have to do to get another US warship to possibly board the *Little Rock*. Not a pretty thought. Lots of levels of senior officers, none of whom Vasquez had much respect or use for. Their pussy-footing might cost the guys on the *Little Rock* their lives. He made a decision and sat down at his desk with the Japanese signal in his hand. For the first time in his life, he broke the chain of command. He wrote a "heads-up" message to Admiral Molly McNamara, Chief of Naval Operations.

When he finished, he walked his message over to the comms office and handed it to the chief in charge.

"Chief, get this on the air ASAP."

"Aye, aye, Sir." Said the chief. Then he looked at the addressee: the Chief of Naval Operations, the head of the Navy.

The chief looked up at Vasquez and said: "Sir? The CNO? You're writing to the CNO?"

"Chief?" Vasquez said putting his face right in front of the chief's face. "Get this message off to Washington right this minute.

"Aye, aye, Sir."

CHAPTER **5**

FLIGHT OPS

"Pete, I've got some work for you." LCDR Bullard said as she entered the office of Commander Peter Dawes, head of flight operations at Diego Garcia.

"One of your boats go missing, Katy? Want my guys to find it for you?" Commander Dawes came back with.

"How the hell did you know?" Katy said stunned, stopping dead in her tracks.

"Know what?" Dawes said jerking upright in his chair.

"That one of my ships is missing."

"No shit? Missing? Really?"

"Well, not physically missing. It's just that we can't contact her. To be exact, we haven't had voice contact with her since 1600 yesterday. And a few minutes after six this morning we got this from a Japanese freighter." Katy said handing the message to Dawes, who slid his glasses down from their forehead perch and read it.

"It's an LCV called the *Little Rock*."

"Pretty strange. And spooky." Dawes said handing the message back. "So, what do you want us to do?"

"The CO ok'd sending an F-18 out to see what's going on. They can slow down enough to get decent visuals, can't they?"

"Sure, not a problem. I'll have fresh duty pilots on at 0800, which is in about 15 minutes." Dawes said looking at his watch. "Why don't you get yourself a cup of coffee and stick around to brief my flyboy.

"Oh, by the way, is the *Little Rock's* nav data working? Otherwise we're going to have a helluva time finding her?"

"Yep, the nav data is working, so you'll be able to home in on her signals. It's just that we've lost voice contact."

Katy got a cup of coffee and went into the Flight Ops briefing room to wait for the F-18 pilot.

I have such a bad feeling. This is really awful. And there I was this morning thinking about Katy Bullard's getting a reprimand instead of thinking about those poor 30-some sailors. God only knows what's happened to them. She thought.

Just then the door opened and a young man in a flight suit entered the room, walked over to Katy, saluted, and said: "Commander Bullard, I am Lieutenant (jg) Peter Krysztof. I'll be doing the search for the ship you're looking for. It's an LCV, the *Little Rock*, isn't it? What can you tell me about her?"

Katy told Krysztof everything she knew about the *Little Rock*, just as she had Captain Vasquez.

As Katie finished, the chief from flight ops entered the room and said to Krysztof. "Sir, the *Little Rock's* nav data seems to be working perfectly. So you should have no problem finding her."

"I'm done here." Katy said. "Good hunting, Lieutenant. When do you reckon you'll be on the *Little Rock*?"

"Two to two-and-a-half hours." Lieutenant Krysztof said, waving his wrist and looking at the chief, who nodded.

"Mind if I come back and listen in when Krysztof gets to the *Little Rock*?" Katy said to Commander Dawes stopping at his office door.

"Where will you be? We'll buzz you when he gets there."

"My office, thanks."

"Katy, don't worry. Peter's one of our best. He'll get the job done."

"Thanks, again." Katy said with a wan smile.

❋ ❋ ❋ ❋ ❋

Katy spent the next two hours looking for ships in the Indian Ocean that might be somewhere near the *Little Rock*. She was in luck.

Vasquez' hunch was right. Not only was there an Arleigh Burke class destroyer doing pirate patrols off the coast of Tanzania, but the *USS Fitzgerald* was now on her way from her post off the coast of Dar es Salaam to the Straits of Malacca on the other side of the Indian Ocean. She should be close enough to the *Little Rock*. And, Arleigh Burkes could make over 30 knots, so the *Fitzgerald* should be able to get there, God forbid they would need to ask her to go.

"Ma'am, it's Flight Ops." One of Katy's petty officers said pointing to the intercom.

"Peter?" She said into the speaker.

"Peter Krysztof has spotted the *Little Rock* and is going down on the deck to take a look." Commander Dawes' voice said.

"I'll be right over." Katy said.

"Peter, Commander Bullard is just now here with me in the comms center. Repeat what you said 60 seconds ago."

"Nobody, M'am. I was all the way down to stall speed. I had a clear look at the bridge. No one. No one anywhere. And that's really crazy, M'am, cuz when we buzz a ship – which we usually get in trouble for doing – everyone pops out to see. Usually everyone who isn't on duty at that very minute comes topside to see the crazy flyboys buzzing their boat."

"Peter?" Katy said, using the lieutenant's first name too. "Did you see anything unusual? Anything at all?"

"That's a negative, M'am. The only thing unusual about this ship is that there's no one out there watching me buzz them. M'am is Commander Dawes still there with you?"

"I'm here, Peter, what's up?"

"Sir, I'm thinking I'm going to give the *Little Rock* a supersonic wake-up call. You, of course, know nothing about this and would never think of authorizing it. I just hope you'll show up at my court martial to cheer me up." You could almost see Krysztof's smile coming through his words.

"Go for it, man, although you didn't hear that from me." Peter Dawes said laughing into the mic.

"I told you he is the best." Peter Dawes said to Katy.

"What was Krysztof talking about? What's he going to do?"

"He's going to go straight up vertical to about 30,000 feet and then he's going down at 90 degrees, full throttle. When he pulls out of his dive, at about 300 feet over the *Little Rock*, he will unleash a sonic boom on that ship that will wake the dead."

"How long will it take?"

"Just long enough for you to fill your coffee cup again." Which she did.

"Hunter One to base." Came Peter Krysztof's voice over the speaker.

"Base here." Peter Dawes said. "What happened?"

"Nothing. Absolutely nothing. I could see my shock wave hit the water. It must have been deafening in that ship. But nobody! There's nobody there looking to see what hit them!

"Commander, Sir, I got a bad feeling about this. I got a feeling that there is not one living soul on that ship. Can't be."

"Ok, Hunter One. You've done a great job. Return to base."

"Oh, dear God!" Katy said quietly.

"Dear God, indeed! What are you going to do now?" Peter Dawes asked.

"There's an Arleigh Burke going from Dar es Salaam to the Straits of Malacca. It's the *Fitzgerald*. They may be close enough to put a boarding party on her. I need to talk to Vasquez. He's got to go to Fleet to get authorization to divert her."

❄ ❄ ❄ ❄ ❄

Katie knocked on the door of Captain Vasquez office. She expected a gruff "come in". Then the door opened and Captain Vasquez stood in front of her. "Oh, it's you, Katy. Come in." Vasquez had a reputation for being a bit formal. It surprised her to hear herself addressed by her first name, rather than her rank. What Vasquez said next surprised her even more. "Why do you go by 'Katy'"? He asked. "Katherine is such a beautiful name."

"Well, Sir." She studdered. "It's because 'Katy' is the name on my birth certificate."

"Well, that certainly explains it." Vasquez said with a broad smile.

"So, what happened with our F-18?"

"Nothing, Sir. Absolutely nothing. The pilot buzzed the *Little Rock* several times and no one came topside to see what was going on. Then, notwithstanding regulations, he dropped a sonic boom on the ship. And, again, no one even stuck a head out a porthole to see what was going on. The pilot was really shaken. So were the rest of us in the Ops Room."

"I know what you mean, Katy." Vasquez said softly. "What now?"

"Well sir, there's an Arleigh Burke, the *Fitzgerald*, that we know is making her way from pirate patrolling off the coast of Dar es Salaam to the Straits of Malacca. She should be close enough to the *Little Rock* to intercept her."

"Hmmh. A guided missile destroyer intercepting an LCV." Vasquez said aloud. "Not a pretty idea. I can't order the *Fitzgerald* to do this. I have to get 3rd Fleet to do it, which ain't going to be easy. But, you're right. It's the only thing we can do.

"Commander, will you prepare the request for me. Just the background on the *Little Rock*, and the *Fitzgerald*, and what all we've done to contact the *Little Rock*. I'll write the begging language myself." Vasquez ended with a smirk.

❊ ❊ ❊ ❊ ❊

"Captain Vasquez, this is Commodore Murton. I'm the new Deputy Commander of 3rd Fleet. I don't think we've met."

"No, Sir. Haven't had the pleasure, Sir." Vasquez said in his best weasel voice.

"Let me get this straight, Captain. You want one of our best guided missile destroyers, the *Fitzgerald*, to intercept and board another American warship – a Littoral Combat Vessel, the *Little Rock*, to be specific? Is that right?"

"Yes, Sir."

"Don't you think that is a little drastic, to say nothing of bizarre and unusual?"

"The way I see it, Sir, is that it's our only option left."

"So, you haven't been able to contact them for almost a day. Did it occur to you, Captain, that their radios might be broken? Sending a guided missile destroyer to board them just might be overreacting a bit, don't you think."

"No, Sir. I don't. Our F-18 buzzed them repeatedly. No one even stuck a head out a porthole to see what's going on. I believe there is something seriously wrong on the *Little Rock*.

"Sir, I know this request is highly unusual. But I am afraid something terrible has happened to the men on board. I think drastic measures are called for. I will take full personal responsibility for this action."

"Indeed you will, Vasquez. Indeed you will.

"Alright, I will take it to the old man and see what he says. I'll be back to you."

"Shithead! Coward! Asshole." Vasquez said aloud when the call ended.

What if these shitheads won't do it? What then? Vasquez thought to himself. Staring out his office window over the calm waters of the Indian Ocean, Vasquez slowly came to the realization of what he would do. If they said 'no', he would go over their heads. He wouldn't go to the next higher authoirity, Central Command in Tampa. He would go directly to the young lady who had the reputation for having the biggest balls in the Navy, the 43-year old Chief of Naval Operations. The bastards at 3rd Fleet would probably court martial him for going over their heads but, by God, let them.

As he was thinking these thoughts, the secure phone rang. It was Commodore Murton.

"The old man thinks you're nuts. But since you are willing to put your career on the line, he has bucked it to Central Command. We'll let you know when we hear back from them."

"Bastards. Assholes! Weasels! Cowards! Shitheads!" Vasquez yelled again when he hung up. "Well they can take it to Central Command or to hell, if they want to." He said out loud. "I'm taking it to the CNO. If I'm going to get court martialed, I might as well get the whole Navy involved." And so Captain Octavio Vasquez, commanding officer of the Diego Garcia US Naval Base – sent another direct message to the Chief of Naval Operations in the Pentagon.

CHAPTER 6

AN UNHAPPY ADMIRAL

Michael Cornell and Molly McNamara had just got back to Molly's yacht, which she parked at a slip on Tyndeco Wharf in Baltimore's cool Canton area. Molly had bought the yacht and moored it in Baltimore because she and Michael didn't want to be seen together in gossipy DC.

Michael had poured them two Rum Chattas over ice, each spiked with a half shot of Fireball. They were sitting in the aft settee on the flying bridge looking over Baltimore harbor and the stars out in the eastern sky. They had just come from a special dinner with Chris Golder, the General Manager of "The Boathouse", the restaurant on the wharf. Chris had been an executive chef most of his career. He was a genius in the kitchen and he had made their dinner of pan-seared sea scallops wrapped in bacon with his special bourbon sauce, himself. At dinner, Molly and Michael had shared a bottle of "Macon Villages", a white burgundy. So, as Molly sat on Michael's lap, they were feeling rested and pampered.

It didn't last long.

Molly's secure cellphone buzzed with an incoming text message. "Damn. I was afraid this would happen." Molly said looking at the message. "I have to check in with the office." She said to Michael getting up off his lap.

Molly went down the companionway to the nav station behind

the helm where she had set up shop with her laptop. She looked at the message that her office had forwarded to her. It was from the base commander at Diego Garcia. He briefly recounted the story of the *Little Rock*, and said that he was sending an F-18 to check her out. *How strange!* Molly thought. She typed in a message for her staff: "Tell Vasquez to keep me apprised every step of the way. I want to know what the F-18 finds out as soon as it happens. Tell him I want to know personally."

"What's the matter?" Michael said as Molly crawled back onto his lap. "Something very crazy." She said. "But I can't bring you in on it."

The two sat there in silence for about 10 minutes when Michael said. "I somehow think our plans to commit an act of marriage tonight have gone astray."

"I'm sorry." Molly said. "I wish I could get away from this damned phone, but I can't."

"I know you can't. It's the job. And it's the job you love. And I love you for your loving it the way you do." Michael said giving her a soft kiss.

So, they finished their drinks and went to bed. About 3 hours later, Molly's phone buzzed again. "I'll be right back." Molly said, touching Michael's cheek gently as she got out of bed.

Molly went back to the upper deck and her computer. A message was there from Vasquez recounting what his F-18 learned and saying that he had requested authority from the 3rd Fleet to order the *Fitzgerald* board the *Little Rock*. Vasquez concluded by saying that the Vice Admiral who commanded the 3rd Fleet had bucked the question up to Central Command and that he was awaiting their decision. *Assholes. Bureaucratic assholes.* Molly thought to herself. *Goddamn crew might be seriously sick or – God forbid – dead, and these assholes won't send someone to find out or help.*

Molly sent a message to her office: Please notify Central Command, the 3rd Fleet, the *Fitzgerald*, and Vasquez at Diego Garcia that the Chief of Naval Operations is, hereby, personally ordering the *Fitzgerald* to intercept the *Little Rock*, and to board her, if necessary, and report her status to all concerned. If boarding is necessary, deploy full MOPP gear. *If there's something evil on the* Little Rock, *I sure don't want it spreading to the whole 3rd Fleet.* Add a thank you to Vasquez for keeping me apprised. Mention that I ordered him to do so, so he won't get burned by 3rd Fleet or CENTCOM.

Molly went downstairs got a couple of allergy pills, a little glass of water, and sat down on the edge of their bed, looking down at the calm and handsome face of the Director of the Ecological and Biological Operations Office (EBOO) at the FBI. She knew Michael was awake. He watched her take the pills.

"Feeling ok?" He asked.

"Yes. They're just allergy pills. I'm just taking them for the diphenhydramine to help me sleep. Not that anything's going to help."

"Seriously bad news?" Michael asked.

"Yes. Something very, very strange has happened to one of our small ships in the middle of the Indian Ocean. We don't know what happened or what's going on out there. So, we're sending another ship to investigate.

"Dear God, I have such a bad feeling about this." She said, looking down at Michael. "You are looking at a very unhappy girl."

CHAPTER 7

THE USS FITZGERALD

Commander Adam Krantz, captain of the *USS Fitzgerald*, was just finishing lunch in the enlisted crew's mess on the ship when a voice came over the intercom: "Captain to the comms center. Captain to the comms center."

"What's up, Nondie?" He said into the intercom box as he got up from the table. "Can it wait? I'm having lunch with some of the guys."

"Captain, we just received a direct order from the Chief of Naval Operations. The lady herself. Can it wait? Your call, Captain."

"Really! From the CNO direct? I'm on the way."

"Gentlemen, time to go back to work. Not every day we hear from the CNO herself." The captain said excusing himself.

❊ ❊ ❊ ❊ ❊

"Well, I'll be damned. Never seen anything like this before." Adam said aloud.

"Yeah, that is pretty crazy." Said Lieutenant (jg) Nondie Hemphill. "Intercept an American warship and board her. I though we were only supposed to do that to pirates.

"Yeah, me too. And, in full MOPP (Mission Oriented Preventative Posture) gear." They must suspect some kind of contamination on the *Little Rock*." Adam said.

"Nondie, get in touch with Diego Garcia and get the nav data frequencies for the *Little Rock*. When you get them forward them to the nav room and tell them to plot and execute an intercept course at flank speed.

"Then ask them for any and all information they have on the *Little Rock*, especially the steps they took to contact her. Then – I am assuming this Captain Vasquez mentioned here is either the CO or the Exec on Diego Garcia – ask if the Captain would stand by for a secure call from me."

Adam went to the bridge, sat down in the Captain's chair and stared out to sea wondering what could have happened to the *Little Rock* – what so important, or tragic, or crazy that the CNO, herself, would get involved? He snapped out of his reverie when Nondie's voice on the intercom summoned him back to the comms center.

"Hmmh." Nondie mused aloud. *Nagamatsu no Mizu*, pretty. It's the name of the Jap ship that tried to hail the *Little Rock*. It means 'water of the eternal – or long-living - pines' in Japanese. Very nice.

"I keep forgetting you speak Japanese." Adam said as he began reading the messages from Diego Garcia. "But then, I guess the Navy sends all of their Japanese-speaking officers to patrol off the coast of Africa. Certainly wouldn't want to send any of them to our bases in Japan."

"I thought they sent me to Africa because I was African-American." Nondie said playing along with the Captain's game.

"Nah." Adam continued absent-mindedly. "They don't have a sense of humor.

"Well, it looks like something really bad happened to the *Little Rock's* crew." Adam said getting serious. "Must have been food poisoning, or something. But what? What could gotten all of them so fast that they didn't even have time to call for help – or let anyone know?

"Maybe, it's something else. Maybe contagious. I guess that's why the CNO said to wear MOPP suits. But, again, what could have happened so fast that they didn't have time to call for help or at least report what was happening. I just don't get it."

"Captain?" It was the voice of the officer of the deck, Lieutenant Commander David Moro, calling from the bridge on the intercom.

"Yes, David." Adam said pushing the intercom button.

"We're locked on to the *Little Rock's* nav data. If they don't slow down, we'll be there in about 3 hours and 45 minutes."

"Ok, thanks, David." Tom said, looking at his watch. That will put us there at about 1900 hours. We'll have another two hours of daylight to complete our mission."

"Uh, Captain, can we ask them to slow down to rendezvous with us?"

"You can certainly try, David. But the reason we're intercepting them is because no one has been able to raise them in the last 24 hours. But, sure, try. Why not? Miracles *do* happen, occasionally."

"Ok, Sir. But if we pursue the *Little Rock* at flank speed, we're not going to have enough fuel to make it to Malaysia."

"We'll deal with the fuel situation once we see what's going on with the *Little Rock*. Oh, and David, would you call Captain Stamatelaky and ask him to join me here in the comms center?"

"Aye, aye, Sir."

"You know." Nondie said. With all of my supposed linguistic ability, I have never been able to place that guy's name."

"Stamatelaky? It's a Greek name."

"Stamatelaky? Greek? Well, I guess that makes some sense. There's a Greek root in there – 'stamato', I think. It means 'stop'. He just doesn't look Greek."

"His father's father married a Filipino woman."

"Ok." Nondie said slowly. "That makes sense. How do you know all this?"

"I asked him what kind of a name 'Stamatelaky' was."

"Oh….."

Five minutes later, the commanding officer of the Marine boarding party detachment, Cpt. Gary Stamatelaky stuck his head into the comms center.

"Gary, looks like we got a job for your guys."

"In the middle of the friggin Indian Ocean?" Gary said in disbelief.

"Yep, and it's not a pirate; it's one of ours."

"Wait a minute, Sir. We're going to board an American warship?"

"We think there may be a serious problem aboard. We need your men to check it out. Your men will need to wear full MOPP gear.

We have received a direct order about this from the Chief of Naval Operations, herself."

"I guess this really is serious then, isn't it?"

"It sure seems so, Gary, my boy."

✿ ✿ ✿ ✿ ✿

It seemed like it took forever for the three hours and forty-five minutes to pass for Commander Krantz, Hemphill, Stamatelaky and the few other people who knew what was happening. Then the shape of the *Little Rock* emerged off the starboard bow.

"Sir?" Gary said to Commander Krantz. "My usual VBSS (Visit, Board, Search and Seizure) team is five marines. Since there's no possibility of hostile fire, we're only going to be three – me and two of my senior gunnies. If there is some contamination – MOPP suits or no MOPP suits – there's no point in exposing any more men than we have to."

"Good call, Gary. Is the chopper ready?

"As soon as you cut the throttle, Sir."

"Three to five, Gary." Adam said looking at his watch. "Good luck and stay safe."

"Will do, Sir."

"Bird's away." The officer of the deck said into the intercom as Adam walked into the comms center.

Adam sat there staring at the flashing lights on the consoles. Didn't even notice when Nondie walked in. After an eternity, Gary's voice came over the radio. "Boarding party to base."

"Go boarding party. This is base. What are you seeing?"

"It's worse than we thought, Captain. They're all dead."

"Oh my God." Nondie said softly, sucking in her breath.

"Captain, it looks like all of these people have been murdered. There are signs of extreme violence. I'm on the bridge. The petty officer here at the helm – a girl – has a hole in her chest, covered with dried blood, as big as my fist. Same with the OOD, who's about 10 feet away. Somebody shoved some big sharp instrument right into both of their chests.

"Down in the galley it's the same. One sailor with a knife sticking out of his eye. Another with a carving knife sticking out of his back. Blood everywhere. Bodies everywhere. This is the worst thing I've ever seen in my life. Jesus H. Christ, Captain, what could have happened?"

"I have no clue, Gary. I have no clue."

"What do we do now, Sir?"

"Let's get you and your men out of there. Be careful not to touch anything. The ship is clearly a crime scene now. Get your men topside. I'll send the chopper back for you."

"Just leave the ship on auto-helm, Sir?"

"Yeah. No point having personnel on board until NCIS or someone can get out here. We'll just sail behind her in case something else crazy happens."

Commander Krantz then composed the most intense and difficult message of his career and sent it off to the Chief of Naval Operations, Central Command, Third Fleet and to Captain Octavio Vasquez on Diego Garcia. He reported that his boarding party had found all 35 crew dead of extreme violence. He reported bodies, body parts and blood all over the ship. He said his men saw no evidence - at all - as to what might have happened. He reported that the *Little Rock* would continue on auto-helm towards Diego Garcia and that he was standing by just aft of the *Little Rock* to support additional boardings by NCIS or other personnel as might be ordered. He asked for further orders.

Adam wondered what would happen next. It didn't take long.

※ ※ ※ ※ ※

"Sir, we've just heard back from the CNO." Nondie said on the intercom.

"I'll be right there."

Hold your position with the "Little Rock". Am ordering preliminary NCIS detail to fly to your ship. Put them aboard the "Little Rock". An NCIS forensics unit is en route to Diego Garcia. They will transfer to your ship. Put them aboard the "Little Rock" too. As you approach Diego Garcia, have your personnel board the Little Rock and put her at anchor off Diego Garcia. We will then await the preliminary report of the NCIS teams. Attention all commands: this matter has been classified "top secret". Please advise any and all personnel with any knowledge of this incident that they are not to speak of it or discuss it with anyone. Tell them it has been classified "top secret". Further orders will be issued by this authority upon receipt of NCIS report. So ordered. McNamara, M., ADM, CNO.

There was one other brief message that followed. Again, it was addressed to all commands. It just said: *Well done, Commander Krantz. McNamara, M., ADM, CNO.*

CHAPTER 8

CAPTAIN GLENN

"Damn." Captain Matthew Glenn said to himself as he looked at the display of his fleet, the "Jutland Fleet", on the wall screen of the Combat Information Center (CIC) of the *USS Enterprise*, Jutland's flagship. He didn't like what he saw. His nine warships had been outmaneuvered by the "Trafalgar Fleet". The *USS Nimitz*, flagship of the Trafalgar Fleet, was swinging into position to launch her aircraft, just as his own planes – low on fuel and vulnerable - were returning to the *Enterprise*, the ship he was on. Jutland and Trafalgar were waging a wargame codenamed "Neverland". Captain Glenn was the wargame coordinator of the Jutland Fleet, commanded by Rear Admiral Robert Gray.

As the Captain stood there staring at the display console, he suddenly realized that something was wrong. Something was seriously wrong. The *Nimitz*, in the middle of making her turn toward his own fleet had overshot her turn. She was now moving away from his own fleet. In a minute, the *Nimitz* would have her stern into the wind, unable to launch her aircraft. It looked like the *Nimitz* hadn't told her escort ships. The cruiser on the inboard side of the *Nimitz* had straightened out as the *Nimitz* should have done too but didn't. The cruiser almost ran into the *Nimitz*. "What the Hell?" The Captain said pushing the comms button.

"Yes sir." Said the Chief manning the intercom in the

Communications Center. "You hearing anything from Trafalgar?" Captain Glenn asked the Chief. "You bet, sir! All hell's broken loose over there. Apparently the *Nimitz* is off course and none of her escorts can hail her. They can't make radio contact.

"I know it sounds crazy, sir, but I think the *Nimitz* has gone dark." Going dark meant shutting off all communications gear. Something no ship would ever do in the middle of a wargame.

"Keep me posted, Chief." The Captain said. "Aye, sir." Came the Chief's response.

Captain Glenn continued to stare at the display as he watched the *Nimitz* who looked like she was going in a circle. A moment later the intercom buzzed. "Yes, Chief?" The Captain said.

"Sir, it looks like some guys on the escorts got in touch with guys on the *Nimitz* by cellphone. They said the *Nimitz* is totally without power. No engines. No steering. No radios. No power at all! The only lights are the emergency battery lights in the passageways.

"They said that when the power went off, the back-up emergency generators started kicking in one-by-one. And then they shut down too! Every goddamn one of the backup generators failed!"

"I'll be damned." Captain Glenn said, more to himself than the Chief.

"Looking back to the display, he could see the *Nimitz* still turning but now clearly slowing down. Just then the intercom buzzed again. "Yes, Chief."

"Sir, it's Commander Mahoney, C.O. of the *Bainbridge*. He requests that you make a secure call directly to him on 7-alpha-alpha-7-7-2."

"Will do, Chief. Thanks very much."

Captain Glenn tapped in the number on the secure phone. "Commander Mahoney, here." Said the voice on the other end.

"Commander, this is Captain Glenn. What's going on?"

"Sir, one of my officers has taken the wargame into her own hands. I thought you and the Admiral should know about it."

"Talk to me, Commander."

"Well sir, we have this comms officer here, Lieutenant Molly McNamara, five years out of the Academy." The Commander said, knowing that Captain Glenn was an Annapolis grad too. "She has a reputation for being a whiz on a computer.

"Well, when the Lieutenant heard my briefing on the status of the wargame – that the *Nimitz* was preparing to launch against us, she got out her laptop and – according to what she told me – she hacked into the internal communications systems of the *Nimitz* and shut off their power. She said all of the *Nimitz'* systems went down. No engines. No steering. No communications. Totally dark.

"And she also said that she could see the *Nimitz'* backup systems starting up. And as each one came on line, she shut those systems down too.

"So, according to my Lieutenant here, sir, the *Nimitz* is dead in the water.

"Sir?" Commander Mahoney went on. "I want to assure you that I knew nothing about this until after it happened and Lieutenant McNamara came to tell me. And, as far as I know, she acted alone and without the knowledge of any of her superior officers. I just want to make it clear that she acted entirely alone and without any orders whatsoever."

Captain Glenn could see what was coming. Instead of being in awe over a stroke of genius, the troops like Commander Mahoney and all of his other officers were circling the wagons, fearing imminent court martial.

"Well, I'll be damned indeed!" Said Captain Glenn to himself with his hand over the receiver.

"Commander?" Captain Glenn said. "Would you order Lieutenant McNamara to pack her bags and strap on a harness. I'm going to send a chopper for her. I want to talk to her right away. Thanks very much."

Dear God, Captain Glenn thought. *A lowly lieutenant. With a lowly laptop. On a lowly destroyer. On a team that was losing a wargame. Completely disables a 101,000 ton warship moving at 30 knots with over 80 aircraft and over 5,000 sailors aboard. Unbelievable! Absolutely unbelievable!* "Court martial her?" He said aloud but to no one. "Hell, I'm going to give her a goddamn commendation!"

❖ ❖ ❖ ❖ ❖

"Admiral Gray, I think you're taking this the wrong way. It's not about winning or losing a wargame. It's about a 28-year old girl who discovered how to disable a major American warship with a goddamn $800 laptop computer! If she could do it, why not the Russians? Why not every gang of terrorist bastards that can scrape up $800? No, sir, this girl doesn't need to be punished. She's got to be sat down and show us how she did it. Then we've got to get her to help us design countermeasures so the Russians and the other bastards can never replicate what she did!"

❁ ❁ ❁ ❁ ❁

"Sir, may I ask you something? Am I in trouble?" Lieutenant McNamara asked Captain Glenn after she had given him a minute by minute account of how she shut down all of the *USS Nimitz'* electrical systems, paralyzing her. She also told the Captain how she figured it all out and how she found the access to the *Nimitz'* systems.

"What makes you think that?"

"As I was unpacking my gear, two MA's showed up. Told me to re-pack my gear, and then brought me here."

"MA's brought you here?"

"Yes, they're waiting outside."

Captain Glenn opened the door and stepped outside. There were two Masters-at-Arms in full uniform. "What's the meaning of this?" The Captain asked them.

"Sir, we were told to escort the Lieutenant in there back to the flight deck when you're done talking to her."

"Who told you to do that?"

The two MA's looked at each other, shocked. "The CO, sir. The orders came direct from the CO."

Captain Glen went back into the room where Lieutenant McNamara was. He held up one finger for her to see – saying "wait" with the gesture. Then he put his one finger over his lips as he picked up the phone and punched in the code for the bridge. "This is Captain Glenn." He said, as a Chief came on line. "Please put the skipper on."

"Peter?" Captain Glenn said as Captain Peter Ross came on. "What's this shit about with the Lieutenant from the *Bainbridge*?" Then he listened.

"Norfolk? What the fuck, man? She's being arrested? She's

probably saved the goddamn ass of the entire United States Navy, and we're busting her?"

"Matthew, listen. This isn't your old buddy, Pete, here, acting on his own. This order came directly from Gray. And he walked in here, himself, to make sure I understood the order. You're saying this is a miscarriage of justice. Ok, I'll give you the benefit of the doubt; but I'm telling you that I have no choice. Lieutenant McNamara is going to Norfolk whether you and I like it or not. Got that? I ain't the goniff here, Matt. It's Gray!"

Captain Glenn hung up and looked at Lieutenant McNamara who was shaking.

"Look, Molly, if I can call you that, what you did was crazy. Pure insanity. But in the course of doing it – and humiliating some brass hats – you showed us exactly how vulnerable the US Navy is to people who can do what you did. People like the Russians and terrorists and others who hate our guts. We need to make sure that none of those bastards can take out their laptops and sink the US Navy, just like you did.

"So, yes, because of a few shortsighted officers with hurt feelings, you are in trouble. But I will get you out of trouble. Believe me, I will get you out of this trouble. I want you to show us exactly how to do what you did. And then I want you to help us build systems that can stop anyone else from doing what you did. Do you think you can do that?"

"Yes, sir."

"And *will* you do that?

"Yes, sir" The Lieutenant said getting some of her composure back.

"Good. Well, you go with the MA's now to Norfolk. But don't worry, I'll be coming right behind you – in the next day or so - as soon as I can get off this tub. Ok? Got that?"

CHAPTER **9**

NCIS

Out of the 2,500 members of the Naval Criminal Investigative Service (NCIS), three of them were stationed at Diego Garcia. When he saw the messages from the CNO, Captain Octavio Vasquez, the base commander, called in the senior special agent Ed McGrath, gave him the official warnings about "top secret" status, and proceeded to tell him about the *Little Rock* and then quiz him about it.

"Oh, wow, Captain, this stuff is way over my pay grade. You gotta talk to Singapore about this, not me."

"That's what I figured. It's over my pay grade too. But I thought I'd ask. Who in Singapore?"

"The Regional Director, Special Agent Luke Dewire."

"Good guy?"

"Don't know him. But from what I hear, yes. A very good guy by all accounts."

"How about forensics?"

"Singapore's got the best. A woman named Thea Alford. She ran the whole forensics show for the entire agency back in Washington. But she says she just got tired of the whole DC scene, wanted to move someplace exotic, and wound up in Singapore."

"Ok, we'll need to get her out here too. But as for now, Agent McGrath, I need to get you out to the *Little Rock*. They've got one hell of a crime scene out there. I need you and your men to take care of it until we can get your people out here from Singapore.

"Chief Menendez?" Captain Vasquez said into the intercom. Please get me Special Agent Luke Dewire at the NCIS office in Singapore."

"Aye, aye, Sir" Came the voice back on the intercom.

A few minutes later Special Agent Luke Dewire, the Regional Director of NCIS for South Asia came on the line. Captain Vasquez gave him the official "top secret" warnings and then told him everything he knew about the *Little Rock* incident.

"In view of the fact that we acting under direct orders from the Chief of Naval Operations, herself, I'd like to ask if you would come out personally, yourself, and take charge of this situation."

"Yes, of course, Captain." Agent Dewire said.

"I understand you have a forensics whiz. Would you bring her too? We have absolutely no clue what happened to those 35 men."

"Yes, Captain. I see Thea's reputation precedes her. That's as it should be. Yes, Captain. She'll be with me."

Getting the NCIS team out to the *Little Rock* would be an ordeal. She was still more than 500 miles out. The NCIS agents were pros. But jumping out of airplanes onto moving ships wasn't their game. The forensics team wouldn't get to Diego Garcia for at least 8 hours. So, since the *Little Rock* was secure, Captain Vasquez decided to wait for the Singapore team to get to Diego Garcia and then land both NCIS units on the *Little Rock* at the same time. The dead sailors on the *Little Rock* certainly didn't care. They weren't going anywhere. And, by that time, the *Little Rock* would be reachable by helicopter. Much better idea.

No one at Flight Ops was prepared for the blindingly bright magenta hair that the young woman on the NCIS flight from Singapore showed up with. "She's Navy? That's regulation hair?" They asked one another loud enough that Thea could hear. She ignored them.

❊ ❊ ❊ ❊ ❊

Forty-four hours later Thea had finished preliminary autopsies on all 35 bodies on the *Little Rock*. All murdered. Random apparent means. She sent her report to Vasquez, who forwarded it up the chain of command all the way to the CNO.

Vasquez sent in a helicopter to take off the NCIS teams and put his own men aboard to put the *Little Rock* at anchor 2 miles west of Diego Garcia. Vasquez asked for a debrief from the NCIS team.

Before the formal debriefing started, Thea asked very loudly to everyone in the room: "What the hell happened to Maguire?"

Everybody in the room looked at each other in amazement. "What?" Vasquez finally said. Just as he opened his mouth, Chief Hernandez' voice came over the intercom. "Sir, message from the CNO."

"Bring it down here, will you Chief? We're in the middle of a debrief."

"Aye, aye, Sir. On the way."

"Ok. Where were we? What did you say, Agent Alford, about somebody named what…Maguire or something?"

"Uh, yeah. Master Chief Petty Officer Andrew Maguire. Anybody know where he is?"

"Who is this Chief Maguire?"

Just as Vasquez asked this, Chief Hernandez appeared and handed him the message from Admiral Molly McNamara, Chief of Naval Operations. The message said: "What happened to Maguire? Did he kill the others?"

"Thea responded to Vasquez, saying: "Captain there were 36 men aboard the *Little Rock*. Didn't anyone notice that there were only 35 bodies?"

"Apparently you and the Chief of Naval Operations did. That's what this message is asking. And it's asking if Chief Maguire could have murdered the others?

"Wow, how did Molly McNamara get in on this? I mean, she has a reputation for being really there, but this is amazing that she is following this case so closely." Thea said.

"It's not often that the Chief of Naval Operations gets news that all of her sailors on a US warship have been murdered." Vasquez said in his best deadpan voice.

"Yeah, well I guess so. But the answer to her question is no. Chief Maguire killed a few of the crew, but not all. His fingerprints were on some of the weapons used, but just a few. There were many different fingerprints on the various murder weapons."

"So, what happened, Agent Alford?" Vasquez asked clearly cutting the debriefing to the chase.

"Can't tell you, Sir. Never seen anything like this. Never even heard about anything like this.

"Sir, I hate to speculate about things I don't know about, but my best guess is that some kind of biological or chemical agent caused these people to murder each other."

"No, wait. You're saying that someone, somehow managed to get a chemical or biological warfare agent aboard the *Little Rock* and use it to cause her sailors to murder each other?"

"Captain, as I said, I have neither seen nor heard of anything like this; but from my investigations, that's exactly what looked like happened on the *Little Rock*.

"Wow, wait till the CNO hears this!"

"You're gonna tell the CNO my speculation about what happened?"

"No. *You* are!"

"Me? I can't talk to her. I'm so tired I can't even think straight."

"I know you are, Agent Alford. I understand you've been up for 48 hours straight. So, our first order of business is to get you some sleep. Then some food.

"I will try to set up a video conference with us and the CNO tonight, when it's morning in Washington. That'll give you plenty of time for sleep and food between now and then. That ok with you, Agent Alford?"

"I guess so, sir. But do I really have to talk directly to Admiral McNamara?"

"Agent Alford, knowing our CNO's reputation, I am sure she would rather hear it firsthand from you than secondhand from me."

"Well, ok, sir."

"Don't worry, Agent Alford, you'll do just fine with our Admiral."

"Ok. Just one more thing, sir?"

"What's that, Agent Alford?"

"Would you mind calling me 'Thea'? Everybody else does. Every time I hear 'Agent Alford', I think of some dreadful chemical like 'agent orange'. Thea works much better."

Vasquez chuckled gently and said: "Of course, Thea. Happy to call you that. And" As his grin widened. "You can call me Captain Vasquez."

Thea smiled broadly. "Deal, Captain Vasquez!" She extended her hand, taking Vasquez clearly aback. But he got over it immediately and they shook hands.

"Now, Captain Vasquez, where can Thea crash for a few hours?"

CHAPTER **10**

GOVERNOR ANTHONY DAY

"Matthew, come in and sit down. How good to see you! Good of you to come. I've needed to talk to you; but I know how busy you were with your dad's funeral – with all of your family and his hundreds of friends. I didn't want to be another burden on you. So, it's great you could come up to Trenton before you head back to your ship."

"Well, it's always good to see you, Governor. You've always been such a great friend of my dad and our whole family. So, I'm delighted you invited me."

"Matthew, what is this 'governor' stuff? Am I supposed to call you 'captain'"? The Governor said with a tone of fake gruffness.

"Well, since the good people of New Jersey gave you such an august title, I thought I should use it, kind sir."

"No, we go back too far. Let's just keep it Matt and Anthony."

"Whatever you say, Governor – uh, Anthony." Matt said grinning. "Seeing you is a breath of fresh air – lots of good memories. Glad I could come. Especially since I'm not sure I'm headed back to any ship."

"Well…. that's actually part of what I want to talk to you about, Matt." The Governor said gently.

"Oh?"

"Yes, your dad told me about your run-in with Admiral Gray."

"He did! How did he know about it? The whole thing was classified top-secret minutes after it happened. I didn't know he even knew about it, much less that he would tell anyone – even a great friend like you, Anthony – because it was so highly classified."

"Well, you know Matt, as Chairman of the Senate Armed Services Committee, your father had any security clearance he needed. And his friends in the Navy certainly weren't going to pick up on a story involving his only son without telling him about it.

"And as far as your favorite Governor is concerned, personally, long before I was Governor, your dad got me appointed to several national security boards and committees that required top secret clearance too. The only rule he and I broke is the "eyes only" rule. We can both be forgiven for that."

"Wow! I didn't know that anybody who wasn't on the flying bridge of one of the two carriers knew squat about what really happened."

"Your young lieutenant gets letters of reprimand from her CO, from her XO, and from the damn fleet admiral. And you write her a letter of commendation." Said the Governor with a chuckle. "That takes big balls, Matthew. Big balls indeed."

"Your father thought that Admiral Gray is an asshole. I don't know the man; but, from what I've heard, I've got to agree. Court martial an officer who exposes a gaping hole in our national defense system? Dear God, we don't need idiots like him in positions of power!

"Amen to that, Anthony. Do you know I had to go all the way to the CNO to get the lieutenant off the hook and into the type of work we need her to be doing. Bunch of brass hats not too happy with that performance – which is why I am not exactly swamped with offers to serve on any decent ships."

"And so, that brings me to why I asked you to come here today."

"It does? I didn't know there was any agenda. I just thought we were going to reminisce about my old man."

"Well, Matthew, you just didn't put your thinking cap on then, did you?" The Governor said with a tone of false seriousness. Yes, there is an agenda or ulterior motive in my asking you here. Let me put it to you directly. I want you to resign from the United States Navy, at which time I will appoint you to your father's seat in the United States Senate."

There was a long pause while both men stared benignly at each other.

Just to break the ice, Captain Glenn turned his head to look full out the window.

"Man, I just don't know what to say. I mean….. I'm so honored. I'm so humbled. I thought I'd never be a patch on my old man's ass. I was hoping to drive a ship until the Lord came for me. Take his place? I'm not worthy."

"Oh yes you are, Matt. To put it bluntly, the reason you didn't shrink from shoving the *Nimitz* business up Gray's ass is because you believed you are right. You believe there is a huge threat to our Navy and our Country from anyone smart enough to hack into our defense systems. And you weren't going to back down. Admiral, or no Admiral.

"You're cut from the same block of granite as your old man. We – no - the Country needs you in the United States Senate.

"Matt, let me tell you that I have shared these thoughts with the President, who thought as much of your father as I did. The President is aware of the *Nimitz* incident and sees it the same way as you and I and your father saw it."

"Really? The President knows about this?"

"Yes, he does. And he's firmly on our side. He has promised that he will do whatever he needs to do to get you onto your dad's old committee.

"Matt, we need you in the United States Senate and we need you on the Senate Armed Services Committee. The Country needs you. We need you to protect us from the stupidity and venality of your colleagues. Can we count on you?"

"Dear God, Anthony, to say I'm overwhelmed is an understatement. Can I have some time to think about all this. I feel like I've been drinking out of a fire hose for the last 20 minutes."

"Sure, Matt. I guess this conversation might have been a little overwhelming if you hadn't expected it, which, clearly, you didn't.

Just don't take too long." The Governor said with a broad smile and a friendly, knowing wink.

❊ ❊ ❊ ❊ ❊

Twenty minutes later Captain Matt Glenn was back on the New Jersey Turnpike heading down to his family's home in Cape May.

When he got to the Garden State Parkway, he pulled over into a commercial plaza. He took out his cellphone and called the Governor's office. The Governor's assistant said he was busy. Captain Glenn told him that the Governor had "ordered" him to call and that the message would take less than 15 seconds. Dumbfounded, the assistant put Matt through to the Governor.

"Governor," Captain Glenn said: "If it is your pleasure, sir, you are now talking to the next United States Senator from New Jersey. I'm in."

CHAPTER **11**

THE VIDEO CONFERENCE

Despite all his years of military training, Vasquez composed his message to the Chief of Naval Operations as if he were talking to his daughter.

Admiral McNamara:

Your question about Chief Maguire was handed to me in the exact instant that the NCIS forensic expert, Agent Elisabeth Alford, arrived in the debriefing room and asked "What happened to Chief Maguire?" Apparently you and Agent Alford were the only people who realized that there were 36 crew on the "Little Rock" instead of 35, as the rest of us swabbies assumed. Agent Alford says that Chief Maguire was responsible for some, but not all, of the murders.

Agent Alford was, apparently, the superstar of the NCIS national lab in Washington before she allegedly got tired of the DC scene and asked to be transferred to Singapore. She is a remarkable young woman. Knowing your deep interest in this matter, Admiral, I would like to suggest that you talk directly with Agent Alford (who, by the way, insists on being addressed as "Thea")

Thea has some definite, if extraordinary, opinions about what happened on the "Little Rock". Better, I think, that you hear what she has to say firsthand from her directly, than secondhand through me.

If you are interested in talking to Thea, who is sleeping now after doing 48 hours of autopsies, etc. on the "Little Rock", I would be pleased to arrange a video conference call at your convenience tomorrow morning.

Please let me know, if this is agreeable to you, and I will arrange it?

And so, after reading it 10 times, and swallowing hard, he sent the message off to the Chief of Naval Operations, Admiral Molly McNamara. *Well* Vasquez thought to himself *at least I used a colon instead of a comma and I didn't begin with "dear".*

Ten minutes later, Vasquez' communications officer reported Admiral McNamara's response: "Do it, Vasquez. 9am EDT, if that works for you and Thea. Please confirm. And thank you."

What a truly remarkable woman! Vasquez thought. *No wonder she's the head of the whole goddamn Navy!*

"Confirm immediately!" Vasquez barked into the intercom.

❀ ❀ ❀ ❀ ❀

"This is Chief Montoya in the CNO's office. Is that you, Captain Vasquez?"

"Yes, Chief, it is?"

"And who is with you there, sir?"

"On my left, Chief, is Special Agent Luke Dewire, agent-in-charge of the NCIS East Asian office. And, on my right, is Special Agent Elisabeth Alford."

"Fine, sir. The Admiral is all ready. I'll get her now."

"How nice you look in your dress uniform, Captain Vasquez!" Thea blurted out as Vasquez reddened totally. "Very distinguished. And all those medals!"

"Well, thank you, Thea. I seldom get compliments around here." Vasquez spluttered.

"Good morning everyone, although I guess it's evening where you are. Ten hours difference, no?" Admiral Molly McNamara said.

"Yes, ma'am. It's 1900 hours here."

"Captain, as you know, I am extremely interested in what happened to the crew of the *Little Rock*. Do any of you mind if I address my initial questions to Agent Alford?"

"Please." Vasquez said gesturing toward Thea.

"Agent Alford, Captain Vasquez has referred to you as 'Thea'. Do you mind if I call you that?"

"Please do, Admiral."

"Good, well let me begin with what is probably the least important question, but one that you and I, Thea, are both interested in: what happened to Maguire?"

"I think he jumped, Admiral. I think he jumped off the *Little Rock* more than 100 miles from land."

"He committed suicide?"

"The more I think about this whole thing, the more I'm sure of it. It fits the pattern perfectly."

"The pattern? What pattern?" Admiral McNamara asked, incredulous.

"Admiral, what do *you* think? Thirty-six well trained, well disciplined sailors start attacking each other for no reason whatsoever? Nope. Something got into those men, something virulent. It produced hysteria and rage. Essentially, they all went crazy together. And they started attacking each other. And they wouldn't stop until everyone was dead.

"My thinking about Chief Maguire is that he was the last man standing. When he couldn't find anyone else to kill, he had to kill himself. And so he jumped into the Indian Ocean miles from land. No chance of surviving. Pure suicide."

"Dear God Almighty, what a story!"

"Tell me about it, Admiral! I've never heard of anything even remotely like this. I keep shaking my head. *This couldn't be so!* But, the evidence all points to the scenario I just described to you.

"Ok, Thea. Let's assume you're right, and I'm sure you are. What could have caused this?"

"Well, Admiral, whatever it was, it had to get into every one of the 36 sailors. So, air, food, or water. Air, on a ship, definitely not. Food, no 36 people eat the same food, and there is no evidence whatsoever that not all of the sailors were affected. I mean even things like butter, you can't count on 100% of people eating. So, it looks like water was the cause.

"This brings us to a totally ugly question. Could any of the 36 crewmen have been a terrorist, or a madman, or otherwise insane enough to commit suicide and take 35 innocent buddies with him?

"Or? Was the poisoning agent – some infected water - introduced into the ship by some foreign party – presumably some kind of terrorist? And, if so, how? When?"

"Thea, can you take some water samples and test them?"

"Oh, I took over a dozen, ma'am. Zippo. Nothing there at all.

"That's why, Admiral, I'm thinking whatever caused these men to go crazy was organic. It was alive. It wasn't just some crazy chemicals. They would always leave their fingerprints behind them."

"Fingerprints?"

"Inorganics, chemicals that is, break down. They break down into simpler compounds. But those simpler compounds – to the extent they're not naturally present in the body – and compounds like this certainly wouldn't be present in the body – would be easy to identify. And, as I said ma'am, I found zippo. No, whatever made those men crazy was alive. And it must have died with them without a trace. Same with the water samples. Whatever living organisms were there died too. Died without a trace.

"Whoa! Holy shit! Oh, sorry, Admiral. I just realized that the toxins in the water had to have died too. But how could they have known when to die?"

"Thea, I'm not following you. What do you mean when you say: 'how could they have known when to die'? What does that mean?"

"Admiral, let's say some micro bugs got into our sailors. Let's say that after a gestation period of, say, 24 hours, the bugs awaken from their dormancy in the sailors' bodies and attack them. Ok, so the bugs know they've been hiding in the sailors warm, well-nourished, very alive bodies for 24 hours and it's time to wake up, attack the sailors, and then die their natural deaths. Ok, you follow me so far?"

"Yes, go on. This is fascinating."

"Well, ma'am, how did the bugs in the water tanks know when to die and disappear? They didn't have any warm body host. No source of nourishment. No symbiosis. Why aren't they still floating around in the water tanks waiting for some unlucky sailor to drink them? I never thought of this till now.

"No. Somehow the bugs in the water tanks knew when to die and how to disappear.

"Admiral, this is the strangest case I've ever heard of. Nothing.

Absolutely nothing even close to this. I really don't know what to tell you other than these 36 poor sailors were killed by one of the most sophisticated biological agents the world has ever seen. But, again, how? When could it have happened? I mean this is a tiny, little ship bobbing around in the Indian Ocean making courtesy calls on nothing countries. Why? What are we missing here? Admiral, I just don't have an answer. I have no clue why these 36 poor men had to die."

"Thea, don't you get down on yourself about this. We don't know all the answers yet. But we know a lot more about this awful situation because of you. So, thank you. I can't thank you enough – for your work and for your thoughtful insights.

"Captain Vasquez, I can't thank you enough for how well you have handled this dreadful situation. I am sorry I have ignored you and Agent Dewire but, as you could see, I wanted to get into the technicals of what happened with Thea.

"Do either of you have anything to add to this incredible story?"

Vasquez and Dewire looked at each other. Vasquez nodded. Dewire said: "Admiral, ma'am, I can only affirm what Thea said. I have never heard of, or read about, anything even remotely similar to what happened on the *Little Rock*. I have no clue, other than that we'd better get down to Mauritius and find our what was going on there when the *Little Rock* was in port. But as to what to look for? Who knows? Known terrorists? Other sinister characters? Who knows what?"

"I take it we're all pretty much in agreement that this was something more than a spontaneous mass murder?" Admiral McNamara asked.

"Oh, for sure." Thea said with both Vasquez and Dewire nodding yes.

CHAPTER **12**

THE POLITICS OF DEATH

"Chief, ask Commander Hamill to come in, please?" Admiral McNamara said to Chief Montoya.

❈ ❈ ❈ ❈ ❈

"Ryan, I need your help with you-know-who."

"Oh, him? What's he done now?"

"It's not what he's done. It's what I want him to do. I need him to do two or three things that he's not really going to want to do. Here." Admiral McNamara said pushing a Top Secret file across her desk.

"Brief yourself on this horrible incident with the *Little Rock*. Have Chief Montoya replay my phone call with this Captain Vasquez, and the video conference with Vasquez and two of the NCIS agents from their Singapore office.

"I need you to write a memo to the Secretary, tell him what has happened, and ask him for three specific orders. One. I want NCIS off the case. Two, I would like NCIS Agent Elisabeth Alford transferred, temporarily, to my office right here. Three. I would like to ask the FBI's Ecological & Biological Operations Office to take charge of the case."

"Jesus H. Christ, Admiral, why don't we ask him to order hell to freeze over too, while we're at it? You want NCIS off the case?

"I take it something awful, involving serious crimes, happened on the *Little Rock*. And you want NCIS *off* the case.

"Exactly, Commander. To be precise, 35 of the 36 crewmembers of the *Little Rock* were murdered - by each other. And the other guy is missing, presumed a suicide. In short, this *ain't* your average murder case. This *ain't* the average NCIS assignment.

"No. Something totally crazy happened on the *Little Rock*. Either terrorists or, worse, a far more organized enemy. But this definitely isn't NCIS territory. It's EBOO territory."

"Ooookaaaay. Well, what about the girl, Agent Alford?"

"She's the only one to figure the whole thing out. I don't mean to bad-mouth Vasquez and the other NCIS people, but, indeed, this Thea Alford, as she calls herself, did figure it all out. I want her right here working with you and me. Got what you need, Ryan?"

"Guess so. I'll get right on it."

"Thanks, Ryan. When you get something, no matter what I'm doing, interrupt me. Ok?"

"Roger that. I'm on it, ma'am."

✻ ✻ ✻ ✻ ✻

"Mr. Secretary, thank you so much for dealing with this important matter so promptly." Admiral McNamara said in a servile voice while rolling her eyes.

"Well, I'm not so sure I'm going to be so prompt in dealing with your proposals." Said Secretary of the Navy, Steven Edward Pannko.

"Oh, well, can I come and talk to you about this?"

"Admiral, there are a couple of other people I need to talk to about this……before it would be appropriate for me to talk to you any further. So, I will get back to you. Good bye."

He's as big a shithead and asshole as everyone says. Molly thought to herself.

✻ ✻ ✻ ✻ ✻

"Goddamn, Mr. Secretary, couldn't we at least fuck up one little bit before you fire us."

"So, Director Swift, you have no problem handling this investigation?"

"Well, Mr. Secretary, I don't think anyone – and I mean anyone, in the FBI or anywhere else – has ever seen a case like this! So, what the hell's wrong with NCIS in the game?"

❊ ❊ ❊ ❊ ❊

"Mr. Secretary! How nice to meet you, even electronically!" Said Gary Gill, National Security Advisor to the President of the United States. "What can I do for you?"

"Mr. Gill, I need to talk to you about a Top Secret matter that involves a dispute between two of my reports."

"A 'dispute between two of your reports'? I'm sorry, sir. I don't follow."

"Mr. Gill, I have a Top Secret matter and a serious dispute between the Chief of Naval Operations and the Director of the Naval Criminal Investigative Service. I need your sage advice."

"Ok, Mr. Secretary, I'm up to my ass in alligators. I'd love to meet with you. Let me get back to you with a time. Ok?"

"Ok, Mr. Gill, I'll wait to hear from you. But Admiral McNamara's in a serious hurry."

"I'm on it, Mr. Secretary. I'll be back to you directly."

Shit. Gary thought, hanging up.

❊ ❊ ❊ ❊ ❊

"So, are you going to meet with Secretary Pannko?" Gary's assistant, Skylar Lasky, asked.

"What makes you think that?"

"Before you got on the line, he was badgering me to set up an appointment with you."

"Well, it seems the good Secretary has a dispute between two of his 'reports' and he wants my 'sage advice'." Gary said making quotes in the air with his hands as he spoke.

"He clearly doesn't know that all of your advice is 'sage'." Skylar said making her own quotation marks in the air.

"I keep forgetting that you made straight A's in Smart Ass in college, didn't you?" Gary said smiling wanly. "Get me Speaker LaFalce's number, will you? I need to do some homework before I get back to your favorite Secretary."

A minute later Skylar yelled "Pick up on 3. I'm dialing the Speaker's office."

"This is Gary Gill, National Security Advisor to President Melissa Daley calling from the White House. I'd like to talk to Speaker LaFalce."

Less than a minute later. "Gary, my boy, how the hell are you doing? Long time no see. Long time no talk."

"Too long, indeed, Mr. Speaker. How the hell have you been?"

"Hanging in here. You know this town. A few moments of gold. The rest, a 'vast wasteland', as a famous former government official once said."

"You know, John, you and I are old enough to know whom you're referring to. But, my assistant, Skylar, for example, super girl, but clueless about 'vast wastelands'."

"Oh, for sure! So what brings us together today, my friend?"

"One of your protégés, I think: Eddie Pannko."

"Oh, dear. Not one of my favorite people. Please don't refer to Eddie as one of my protégés. I'd like to stay friends with you." They both laughed.

"Eddie wants to talk to me about a dispute between the head of NCIS and Molly McNamara."

"Let me give you a little background on our boy, Eddie." Speaker LaFalce said.

"Our friend has an interesting history. Grew up in the Polish neighborhoods of Chicago. Dad, Edward Pannko. Mom, Tanya Polanski. Although his given name is 'Steven', he likes to be called 'Eddie'.

"Eddie went to college in Milwaukee and liked it there. After college, he got married – to a local Polish girl.

"We Italians have a cultural organization, The Sons of Italy. The Polish guys have their own organization called the 'Polish Falcons'. Their local lodges, or whatever, are called 'Nests'!

"So, our pal, Eddie, gets active in Polish Falcons, Nest 6. He runs for president and wins. Then he runs for Congress using the Polish

Falcons and the whole Polish community in Milwaukee as his power base. He wins.

"He does this for 25 years. AND, during those 25 years he never misses an opportunity to get every possible nickel of federal money sent back to Milwaukee.

"He winds up on the House Armed Services Committee. There he finds every federal dollar that can go to any place that any of his fellow committee members represent. He becomes 'Eddie Largesse'.

"In return for all of this gratuitous largesse, Eddie gains the loyalty – and the votes - of the members of the committee. So, Gary, you understand, Eddie can deliver the votes. And, that's what the White House and I need – someone who can deliver the votes.

"Now the scene changes back to Milwaukee. One year a young upstart arises who wants to challenge Eddie for president of Polish Falcons Nest 6. This young kid has a genealogical check done on Eddie. Guess what? The study shows that Eddie's father's people aren't from Poland; they're from Finland! Eddie's father died when he was young. His mother was 100% Polish. So, Eddie was raised by his 100% Polish family and truly believed that he was 100% Polish.

"No shit. After all those years?"

"Exactly. So Eddie proceeds to lose the Polish Falcons election to the young kid. Then, a few months later, Eddie apparently sees some handwriting on the wall to the effect that his days in Congress are numbered too. So, he packs up his baggage, which is all that he has done for me and the White House as a committee chairman, and comes to cash in his chips. He says to me: 'call the President and see what you two can do to reward all my years of devoted service'. So, that's what I did. And between President Daley and me, we figured Eddie could do only minimal damage to our Republic as Secretary of the Navy. So, there you are. That's where Navy Secretary Eddie Pannko comes from."

"What a great – if frightening – story."

"Listen, Gary, one more thing. If Eddie has a problem between the Navy and the NCIS, I'd strongly suggest you talk to Matt Glenn. First, as chairman of the Senate Armed Services Committee, Matt sat across the table from Eddie at every Conference Committee meeting for the last 10+ years. He knows Eddie better than I do.

"Plus, as you may know, Matt has been Admiral Molly McNamara's rabbi for the last 15 years."

"Rabbi?" Gary said quizzically.

"I love that expression, rabbi. The boys from New York City use it. It means 'godfather' – you know – someone who watches out for and takes care of someone. The story has it that the big brass hats in the Navy wanted to court martial Molly for some cyber stunt she did that embarrassed the hell out of a lot of them. Matt blocked the court martial and got her promoted every other year so that she could teach the Navy what cyber warfare is, how to do it, and how to defend ourselves against it.

"You think Eddie Pannko's story is cool. Molly's is much cooler. And, of course, she's now the head of the whole goddamn Navy. And, rumor has it that the distinguished President of the United States, our friend, Ms Daley, wants to make Molly the Chairman of the Joint Chiefs of Staff, the highest ranking officer in the entire United States Military – at the age of 43! Can you believe it?

"Funny you should say that, John. I believe I've heard that rumor too."

"I'll bet you have."

"Yes, every now and again our Commander-in-Chief starts ranting about getting Molly to drag the other services kicking and screaming into the "Cyber Age", just like she did the Navy. All very amusing when you hear it, but I'll bet you it happens next time the joint chiefs' chairman retires."

"Probably so. But, my friend, the best advice I can give you on your Eddie Pannko issue is to talk to the distinguished Senator from New Jersey, Mr. Glenn."

"Thanks very much, John, I will give him a call right now. So long, and take care of yourself.

"You too, Gary."

❋ ❋ ❋ ❋ ❋

"Sky, can you get me Senator Glenn's phone number?"

"Am I actually talking to the very distinguished National Security Advisor to the President of the United States?" Senator Matthew Glenn, Chairman of the Senate Armed Services Committee said tongue-in-cheek to Gary when he came on the line.

"Oh, Mr. Chairman, the honor is all mine." Gary said in the same mock tone of voice."

"What brings you to call this lowly public servant from the great State of New Jersey?" Matt said continuing along with the funny talk.

"It is about three friends of yours."

"Three friends of mine. I didn't know I had three friends."

"Our Speaker of the House says you do: Molly McNamara, Tim Swift, and Eddie Pannko."

"Well, guilty as charged. I certainly know Molly and Eddie and I have dealt with Swift enough times. What's the problem with these three?"

"Well, Matt, we have a very serious, very top secret situation with a Naval vessel in the Indian Ocean. I will messenger you over the brief top secret memo that describes this unbelievable situation.

"But essentially very serious crimes were committed on this ship. Admiral McNamara does not believe they were run-of-the-mill, normal type crimes. She believes they were the work of terrorists or madmen. She says this is not a case for NCIS. She wants to bring in the FBI's Ecological & Biological Operations Office."

"The head of that office is her boyfriend, isn't it?"

"Yes, that may complicate the matter."

"Well, I'll be damned. I wonder what Molly's problem is. I mean NCIS is no match for the scientific expertise of the EBOO. But, they're certainly good at police work. I mean, Gary, it seems to me that its one thing to figure out what happened. Sure EBOO is probably real good at that. But, then there's the problem of catching the guys who did it; and I gotta believe NCIS is real good on that side of the matter. Why can't they all work together?

"I don't know, Matt. Perhaps they can."

"You know, Molly, Swift and Michael Cornell are all three peas in a pod. Molly is, of course, Academy. Cornell – despite his distinguished name – is prep school and then Georgetown. And Tim

Swift is prep school and then Colgate. They all gotta get along. Their birds of a feather."

"You call Swift, 'Tim'?"

"Yep, that's what everyone who knows him calls him. His proper name is Harlan Justin Swift, but he goes by Tim. Funny, he says he has no clue where the name 'Tim' actually came from. His mother told him that one of his nannies thought that 'Harlan Justin Swift' was just too big a mouthful to call a little tyke. So, the nanny apparently started calling him 'Tim' and it stuck. Anyway, from my dealings with him, he seems like a super guy. I am sure he and Molly would get along famously. That goes for Cornell too. They're all three alike."

"In that case, Matthew, my friend, may I ask you a favor?"

"Whenever you refer to me as your 'friend', I know there is evil afoot. What favor?

"To hell with our Secretary Pannko. I'll blow him off. But I'd like to get Molly and Swift and Cornell into the same room and get them to work together. God knows that when you read the classified document about this case, you'll see how important it is and why they should all cooperate and work together. But, I may need your help in persuading them.

"Molly, as you know, has a reputation for being headstrong. But she certainly would listen to you. Swift certainly isn't going to say no to you either. I know Cornell reasonably well; but I know Jim Slevin, the newly appointed Director of the whole FBI, very well. I can talk to Jim and make sure he softens up Cornell.

"So, what say you, Mr. Chairman? Can I persuade you to leave your aerie at the Capitol and come down to the White House for a meeting with these three?"

"Yes. That I can do. Are you inviting my favorite Jersey Girl too?"

"You know, Senator, even though you are both from the same state, if you call our distinguished president "Jersey Girl" in public, she will have you shot."

"Yeah, either that or Kevin Smith and the Hollywood people will shoot me. But what about your calling her "Missy"? She going to shoot you too?"

"I would never call her that in public. Or, she probably would shoot me."

They both laughed.

Ok, speaking of shooting, let's shoot for a meeting tomorrow right here in my office. I'll have my assistant, Skylar, call everyone and set it up. That sound ok to you?"

"Yep, my schedule's pretty flexible tomorrow. So, as I said: that I can do."

✻ ✻ ✻ ✻ ✻

Skylar got back in touch with the Secretary of the Navy and invited him to Gary's office in the White House that afternoon.

When Secretary Pannko arrived, Skylar ushered him into Gary's office with great pomp and ceremony. She got him a diet coke and made him feel at home. A few minutes later, Gary entered and did the same thing – made Secretary Pannko feel very much at home. Gary asked him about growing up in Chicago. He asked about Pannko's career in Milwaukee with the Polish Falcons and his many years in Congress. Eddie was feeling very relaxed and so told Gary several long-winded, relatively pointless stories that made Gary desperately want to keep looking at his watch – but he didn't.

Finally, Gary said: "These stories about your career are all great fun, Mr. Secretary; but what do we need to do about the matter at hand with NCIS and the CNO?"

At that, Secretary Pannko launched into a long summary of Molly's career. Then he cited chapter and verse of all of the great investigations that NCIS had done. Then he needlessly denigrated the FBI's EBOO. At the conclusion of all these often shapeless gales of wind, the Secretary allowed as how he was disinclined to grant Molly's request to back off the NCIS and replace them with the EBOO. The Secretary had learned that Michael Cornell at the EBOO was Molly's boyfriend. The Secretary – with a straight face – said he thought this was unseemly nepotism.

At the end of the Secretary's remarks, Gary walked to the window and rubbed his mouth a couple of times. Then he turned to Secretary Pannko and said: "Mr. Secretary, I don't know if you are aware of it or not, but the President of the United States is very fond of Admiral McNamara. She also knows Michael Cornell at the FBI, and is fond of him too.

"So, Mr. Secretary, I would say that if you tell Admiral McNamara that she cannot call in the FBI on this case, the Admiral will have her letter of resignation on the desk of the President of the United States within the hour.

"When that happens, Mr. Secretary, I can assure you that the President will not accept Admiral McNamara's resignation." A brief, ominous pause, and then: "But she will ask for yours. Do I make myself clear, Mr. Secretary?"

The Secretary sat there stunned for several long seconds.

"So, what do I do, Mr. Gill? Fire NCIS? Tell them to stay the hell away from the case?"

"Mr. Secretary, let me make a recommendation to you. Let me handle this matter."

As Secretary Pannko was about to object, Gary held up his hand to stop him.

"Mr. Secretary, the President has been briefed on the *Little Rock* incident. She has given explicit instructions that she wants to be kept in the loop about what we're going to do about it. And, she has charged me, personally, with keeping her informed. So, you see, Mr. Secretary, I am going to be in the middle of this matter whether any of us like it or not.

"So, I advise you, sir, to let me handle this matter between the CNO, the EBOO and NCIS. Somehow I will manage to keep peace in the family while making sure the investigation is successful and we get to the bottom of this tragic mess. Do I have your agreement on that? I will handle the matter between the CNO, the NICS and the EBOO from now on, right? And you will not concern yourself with this matter any further? Please tell Admiral McNamara and Director Swift that they will be hearing directly from me today. Is that clear, sir?"

"Yes." Secretary Pannko said looking at his shoes. "It's clear."

"Thank you, Mr. Secretary, for all your effort and concern on this delicate matter." Gary said as he ushered Pannko to the door.

❄ ❄ ❄ ❄ ❄

"Sky, will you get a hold of Admiral McNamara, the NCIS Director, Tim Swift, Michael Cornell at the FBI, and Senator Glenn and organize a meeting for the five of us here in this office tomorrow afternoon? And, will you get me Jim Slevin's new number at the FBI right away. I need to talk to him about Cornell."

"I'll get right on it." Skylar said.

"By the way, I am such a fan of Secretary Pannko's that I did a little eavesdropping on your conversation. Your line: 'Mr. Secretary, the President of the United States will not accept Admiral McNamara's resignation. Instead she will ask for yours.' was totally brilliant. If they gave Academy Awards for government speeches you would certainly have won one with that line."

"Ah, yes, Ms Lasky. I had forgotten that you were a drama major in college. It's nice to be appreciated." Gary said with a big grin.

CHAPTER **13**

BUILDING THE TEAM

"Hello, this is Gary Gill, National Security Advisor, calling for Jim Slevin. Is he there?"

"No, I'm sorry, Mr. Gill, Mr. Slevin is out. We expect him back in about an hour."

"Listen, I am sending Jim a top secret memorandum that I would like him to read as soon as he gets back and then call me. Would you ask him to do that?"

"Certainly, Mr. Gill."

❖ ❖ ❖ ❖ ❖

"It's Jim Slevin." Gary's assistant, Skylar Lasky, yelled from the outer office when Slevin called back.

"Good God, man! What the hell happened to those poor bastards on the *Little Rock*?" Slevin said before Gary could even say hello.

"That's the question of the hour. Listen, I need your help on this matter."

"Sure, what's up?"

Gary then explained to Slevin that Molly McNamara thought it was a far more sophisticated crime than NCIS was used to dealing with so she wanted to take them off the case and replace them with EBOO. He went on to say that he was having a meeting the following afternoon and that Michael Cornell, NCIS Director, Tim Swift,

Admiral McNamara and Senator Matt Glenn would all be there. He said that Senator Glenn thought that there was enough work for everyone on the case. EBOO was probably good at finding out what happened. But that NCIS would certainly be good at catching the bad guys. So, Gary and Senator Glenn hoped that they could get Molly and Michael and Swift all working together.

"Can you help me with that?" Gary concluded.

"Yeah, I agree with Glenn. Those three are like peas in a pod."

"I think that's the exact phrase Matt Glenn used."

"Listen, Gary. You know I think the world of Mike and Molly. Well, this guy Swift is the same kind of guy. Do you know what he did, like the week after he was confirmed by the Senate? He calls me. He asks to come over and talk. So, he comes over and tells me he's afraid he's in way over his head and asks if I mind if he calls me from time to time for advice. I thought to myself *what the hell is a guy with that much humility doing in Washington*? Well, of course, you can call me anytime, I told him. Then we just shot the breeze for about an hour.

"Swift is a very interesting guy. A Buffalo boy. I'll bet John LaFalce knows either Tim or his family. Tim's old man went to Colgate then Yale Law, then he became a partner in a big Buffalo law firm and then he went on to be the President of the Erie County Savings Bank up in Buffalo. Tim went to the local prep school in Buffalo, then followed in his father's footsteps to Colgate. There, however, partying got the better of him. They asked him to leave. Then he joined the Navy as an enlisted man and served four years. Then back to the local state college in Buffalo for a degree.

"While in college, Tim got interested in politics. When he graduates he gets elected to the City Council. Get this – as a Democrat! Can you imagine coming from an old line WASP Republican family, and he registers Democratic. Go figure. Anyway, at this time the famous Daniel Patrick Moynihan is making his first run for the U.S. Senate in New York. Tim becomes Moynihan's campaign manager.

"After Moynihan wins, he wants Tim to come to DC. But Tim wants to stay in Buffalo. So now he runs for the Erie County Legislature and wins. Then he becomes chairman of the Legislature's Criminal Justice Committee. A couple of years later, he is appointed

Commissioner of Central Police Services for Erie County. Finally, a few years later, Moynihan's chief of staff leaves for another job. Moynihan finally persuades Tim to move to DC and go to work for him. So, as you know, Moynihan finally decides to retire last year. Tim doesn't want to go back to Buffalo now. So, he and Moynihan go over Tim's resume. First, there's the Navy, then there's the Criminal Justice Committee in the Legislature, and finally there's the Commissioner of Central Police Services job. As it turned out at the time, the NCIS job was vacant. Moynihan calls the President and next thing you know Tim is up talking to Matt Glenn about getting confirmed by the Senate. Isn't that a hell of a story?"

"It really is. I can see what you and Matt Glenn mean about Tim, and Michael and Molly all being able to work together.

"Listen Jim, can I persuade you to attend the meeting tomorrow afternoon? You know Michael. You know Molly. And you know Tim Swift. Plus, I think we are probably going to need more than just EBOO and NCIS working on this case. I can imagine other parts of your operation will get involved too. So, it would probably be a good thing for you to be there – not just to keep the peace – but to participate directly and completely. What say you?"

"I was hoping you'd ask me. I think this is the most fascinating – and unbelievable - case I have ever seen or heard of. I'd love to be personally involved."

"Great. I'll have Skylar get back to you with the meeting details. Done."

"Double G, there's one more thing I think we need here. We need a listener. We're going to start generating leads, I am sure. We're going to track down every living soul that came within a hundred yards of the *Little Rock*. When we do, we will need to find out whom these people are talking to and what they're talking about."

"You're thinking NSA?" Gary asked.

"Exactly."

"Good call. Let's see." Gary said walking over to the window.

"Slev, you know Alison Murphy don't you?"

"Don't think so. Who's she?"

"She's the number 3 at NSA. She's their chief listener, so to speak.

She's head of F-6, the Special Collection Service. All the cyber people report to her. Molly knows her."

Isn't "Special Collection Service" the damnedest name you've ever heard of?" Slevin interjected. It is actually a special collection of all of the cyber spooks in this government."

They both laughed.

"Why do you think I should I know this Ms Murphy?"

"She's a New Yorker like you."

"Really she's from New York?"

"Well, Brooklyn. Close enough."

"No, Double G. Not close enough. How many times do I got to tell you that Brooklyn ain't New York. They're two entirely different countries."

"Fine. Fine. Anyway, you're both from the lands east of the Hudson River.

"You'll like her Jim. She's your kind of person. As a matter of fact, she's very much like her friend Admiral Molly McNamara. So, she'll fit right in with Molly and Swift and Michael Cornell."

"As the saying goes, 'any friend of yours' Double G. I'll look forward to meeting her."

"Great, I'll have her at the meeting here at the White House."

❖ ❖ ❖ ❖ ❖

Gary decided that, since the President personally knew all of the people at the meeting, except Swift, that he would brief her on what he had in mind.

"I'm glad you're telling me this, Gary. I have a real bad feeling about this *Little Rock* matter. I certainly agree with Molly that this is far more than your average run-of-the-mill mass murder. And I agree with you and Glenn that there's more than enough work here for everybody, Alison included. We've got to get them all working on it, and we've got to get them working together. This is absolutely the last place we need office politics or turf wars.

"Listen, why don't you have the meeting right here in my Cabinet Room. I think when these folks realize where they're meeting, they'll be more likely to lay aside any petty grievances."

"Good idea, Ma'am." Gary said.

"And." The President went on. "After you read them the riot act about working together, why don't you press the little "POTUS" button under the table. That'll be my signal to come in. I will personally remind them of the consequences of not working together. Nobody's going to repeal the riot act as long as I'm in this chair." The President said with a smile.

"Super, Missy! That's exactly what we'll do." Gary concluded.

"Gary? I've told you not to call me Missy. People will catch on about us. No one calls the President by her first name unless they are family. And you aren't there, my friend – at least not yet."

"Yes, Madam President." Gary said with mock seriousness. They both smiled at each other.

※ ※ ※ ※ ※

Melissa Armstrong Daley, Ph.D. had taken an unlikely path to the White House. While in graduate school at Columbia University, she met Tom Daley who was in law school there. They married and settled in Trenton, New Jersey, where Tom was from. Missy, as she was called, got her Ph.D. in special education. She went to work for the Camden Board of Education. There were a lot of special ed needs in Camden and not a lot of money to address them. Camden was a 35-mile commute from Trenton. But Missy left early each morning, so the drive took only 40+/- minutes. Tom practiced law and got into politics, which was his real love.

Tom was elected Mayor of Trenton and then Governor of New Jersey. In the middle of his second term as Governor, the senior U.S. Senator from New Jersey died. Tom made a deal with his Lieutenant Governor. Tom would resign as Governor so that his deputy would become Governor. Then the new Governor would appoint Tom to fill the vacant seat in the U.S. Senate. This was only the 10th time in U.S. history that this had happened.

So, Tom was first appointed to the Senate but was then reelected three times in his own right. Missy continued to teach in Camden. They saw each other on weekends.

Shortly after his second term began, tragedy struck. Tom was stricken with amyotrophic lateral sclerosis (ALS), or Lou Gehrig's Disease, the same one that felled Professor Stephen Hawking. The disease quickly intensified. Missy had to resign. She moved to Washington to take care of Tom. Over the course of the next 12 years, as Tom got progressively weaker, Missy took on more and more of his responsibilities. The word in the inner circles of the Nation's Capitol was that Missy was the real Senator from New Jersey. If you needed something, go directly to her, not Tom. So, when Tom eventually died, it was no surprise that the Governor of New Jersey appointed Missy to fill his seat.

Ten years after Missy became a Senator, the national Democratic Party was about to self-destruct over a bitter primary battle between rivals for the presidency.

Then there was Senator Melissa Armstrong Daley, doctor of special education. She had worked for many years among the underprivileged children of Camden. Then she resigned to take care of her sick husband. Then, when he died, she succeeded him in the U.S. Senate where she was gained a reputation as a brilliant, hard-working, resourceful, and well-respected legislator, whom everyone liked.

What better candidate for President could the Democrats ask for? And a woman, too!

The people agreed. And so, Dr. Melissa Armstrong Daley became the 47th President of the United States.

CHAPTER 14

MUNICH

To most observers Mustafa al-Khalid looked like an average middle-aged faculty member at the venerable Ludwig Maximilian University (LMU) in Munich. On decent weather days he rode his bicycle across the English Garden to the University, just like other faculty members and thousands of students did every day. Cars were out of the question at LMU. No place to park at any price. Even the University's own fleet of maintenance vehicles often had to park blocks from where they were working.

Mustafa prided himself on his ability to blend into the University community with the bicycle and drab faculty garb. Although he did choose a leather messenger bag over the typical canvas backpack that everyone else at the University – both faculty and students - preferred.

Mustafa actually prided himself on being able to blend in with the general public, too. Unless it was seriously inconvenient to do so, or the weather was inclement, Mustafa walked, bicycled, or took public transport wherever he went. And his attire looked strictly "consignment store". So too was his taste is restaurants and bistros. In fact, Mustafa – especially when he was doing "business" - actually preferred the tourist venues, of which there were many in Munich.

Mustafa preferred the tourist areas for what he thought was the anonymity they provided him. Who would recognize him in a sea of faces changing daily? He wanted to be anonymous.

What he didn't realize was that there is an opposite phenomenon. The staff at all of these tourist places were the same every day. Every day they looked out over a sea of unknown faces none of whom they had ever seen before. None, that is, except the very few regular customers, who stood out. As Mustafa would seat himself in the giant Hofbräuhaus for a meeting with agents of the *Stiftung Erдlust*, a dark foundation with whom Mustafa did business, the wait-staff would say to each other: "Look, Teur'Tasche is back." They identified Mustafa by his most stand-out characteristic, his expensive – and uncharacteristic – satchel. So much for anonymity.

The place where Mustafa shed all his pretensions of the commonplace was at his home.

Across the English Garden from the University ran the River Isar. And along the western bank of the Isar ran the elegant Widenmeyerstrasse in the equally elegant Lehel District.

Mustafa owned the fifth and top floor apartment at #45 Widenmeyerstrasse. Elegant, yes. Opulent, yes. Mustafa shared his mother's taste for expensive furnishings. The important rooms in the apartment all faced East. They all had magnificent views of the Isar. The apartment had high ceilings and a fireplace in the living room that a grown man could walk into without bending over. Above the mantle was a large masterful painting, which said much about the personality of its owner. It was a painting of the Blue Mosque. But it was a watercolor. Paintings of mosques were wildly popular everywhere in the Middle East and the Muslim world. But watercolors in those countries were rare. Watercolors were popular in Japan and all over the West. This was Mustafa's bifurcated personality. His heart was in Istanbul; but his head was in Western Europe. It was this strange affinity for things western – like his love of the Latin and Greek literature and culture that he taught – that drew him to the delicacy of watercolors.

Beneath the painting was a large photograph of a young man and woman who looked exuberantly happy. It was Mustafa and the only woman he ever loved, Jasmine. The picture was taken at their engagement party on Mustafa's family's yacht off the coast of Kusadasi a dozen years ago. It captured – literally – the last moment that Mustafa had ever seen Jasmine alive. Just after the photographer snapped the shutter, Jasmine turned away to speak to an older relative. It was at that precise second that the US Navy's Hellfire missile, fired from a Reaper drone hovering above, struck the yacht. It killed almost all 54 people on the yacht. That included Jasmine and all of her family and most of Mustafa's family. It maimed Mustafa, scorching much of the skin on his face. It took six bouts of cosmetic surgery before Mustafa even felt remotely like going out in public without covering his face.

Mustafa liked to look at the photograph every day for two reasons. Jasmine, of course. And, the United States Navy.

❊ ❊ ❊ ❊ ❊ ❊

Into Mustafa's quiet and unruffled academic life one day, Dr. Nicola Angelini, Mustafa's best friend dating back to the first days of high school, showed up – unexpected - in his lavish apartment in Munich. Nicola had lots of luggage with him. Too much.

Nicola explained that he needed Mustafa's help in starting a new life in Germany. He told Mustafa that the Swiss authorities had forced him out of the country. But instead of telling Mustafa how he sedated his patients and then extorted huge sums of cash out of them, he lied and said how successful his experimental treatments were and that the Swiss authorities were indignant and jealous that Nicola was diverting patients from government-run medical programs. Nicola even showed Mustafa his Swiss medical credentials and assured him that the German government would honor them and allow him to practice medicine in the country. Nicola asked if he could stay with Mustafa until he got back on his feet. Mustafa's apartment was a large three-bedroom suite, and Nicola was his best friend in the world; so, of course, he said yes.

CHAPTER **15**

THE CABINET ROOM

As each person showed up for the meeting, Skylar Lasky greeted them with uncharacteristic formality and escorted them into the large waiting room outside Gary Gill's office where she asked that they remain until all of the attendees were present at which time she would escort them to the Cabinet Room. Sky noticed that as she said "Cabinet Room", a little light went on in each visitor's eye.

The group broke into cliques. Admiral Molly McNamara and FBI Agent Michael Cornell paired off in one corner. NCIS Director, Tim Swift and FBI Director Jim Slevin gravitated to another where they were joined by Senator Matt Glenn.

Slevin figured that the only one missing was Alison Murphy from the NSA. But just then the door opened and a pretty young girl with magenta hair appeared in the doorway with Skylar.

"Who the hell is that?" Slevin mumbled under his breath.

"I'll introduce you." Tim Swift choked as NCIS Special Agent Elisabeth Alford walked over to their group saying: "Hi, Director Swift. I knew you'd be here."

"Thea, how did you get here?" Tim blurted out. "As if I didn't know." He finished under his breath. "Oh, Thea, let me introduce you. This is FBI Director Slevin and this is United States Senator Matt Glenn from New Jersey.

"Gentlemen, this is Special Agent Elisabeth Alford."

"A pleasure to meet you, Agent Alford." Senator Glenn said. "Likewise." Jim Slevin echoed.

"Nice to meet both of you gentlemen." Thea said demurely and then turned to wave at Admiral McNamara who waved back mouthing the words "Hi, Thea."

A few moments later, when Alison Murphy entered the room, Jim Slevin went over and introduced himself. "I understand you come from the City." (People born and raised in NYC felt no need to identify it more than just saying "the City", as if there were no other cities in the world.)

"Well I did." Alison said smiling. "I went to Syracuse for college and just gravitated down to the City to work for several years and get my Ph.D. in communication technology at NYU."

"So you're not from the City?" Slevin asked emphasizing the word 'from'.

"No, I'm actually a Maryland girl. So, now that I'm at NSA, I'm back in my element."

"Are you a New Yorker?" Alison asked using a phrase that no one from "the City" would ever use.

"Yep." Slevin said wincing. "Born and raised in Queens. Villanova for college and then back to Fordham Law School with a stint with the NYPD thrown in." He said affably.

Just then, the door opened at the other end of the room and in walked the National Security Advisor to the President of the United States, Gary Gill.

"Gentlemen and ladies." Gary said with a slight nod to Admiral McNamara, Alison, and Agent Alford.

"I know most of you, but let me introduce myself to the two folks I don't know."

"Tim." Gary said walking toward Swift. "Nice to meet you, finally."

"And." He continued turning toward Thea. "This must be Special Agent Elisabeth Alford." He said smiling broadly. And then he said: "Better known in most circles as 'Thea', I understand.

"Did I get that right, Thea?" He said laughing.

"Nailed it, sir." Thea said holding her thumb up. Everyone joined in the laughter.

"Ladies and gentlemen," Gary said. "Thea is a forensic scientist for NCIS. She has been aboard the *Little Rock* and examined each of the bodies there. Thea knows more of the details of this case than any of us. That's why we invited her to join us.

"As I think you know, we will be meeting in the Cabinet Room." Gary went on. "President Daley, herself, directed that we meet there as an indication of the importance she attaches to this matter."

A shiver of foreboding passed through the little group.

"Skylar, will you lead us to the Cabinet Room now?"

And so Skylar Lasky escorted Gary Gill and the six visitors up through the West Wing and into the Cabinet Room.

❀ ❀ ❀ ❀ ❀

"Admiral, it's your ship, and you've known about this the longest. Why don't you tell us what you know?" Gary began.

Since everyone else in the room had learned whatever they knew from either Thea or Molly, they obviously dominated the conversation for the next hour and a half. During that time – especially when Thea was describing how certain of the crewmen were murdered - there were several audible breath-suckings and two "Dear Gods", all of which emanated either from Slevin or Senator Glenn. A palpable shiver went through the entire room when Thea described how the young woman petty officer manning the helm was impaled at her post with a blunt rod.

"Let me see if I can summarize, if that's alright with you, Gary?" Molly said finally.

"Please do, unless anyone has any questions?" Gary said looking around quizzically.

"I'll wait till the Admiral puts it all together." Slevin said.

"'Putting it all together.' That's certainly a major overstatement." Molly said.

"The bad news is that we have 35, or most certainly 36, dead sailors, all of whom murdered each other, or, in the case of Maguire, committed suicide. The worse news is that we have absolutely no idea why they did this. And the worst news of all is that – despite Thea's heroic efforts in the laboratory – we have little or no evidence at all as to what could possibly have caused these men to turn on their comrades and murder them. Clearly they were all out of their minds. But what caused that? What made them all go crazy simultaneously? We have absolutely no idea!

"Thanks to Thea, we believe we are dealing with a virus. But if it is a virus, as Thea is the first to admit, it behaves like no other virus anyone has ever seen."

"What makes you think it's a virus?" Slevin interjected, turning to Thea.

"It acts like a virus, Mr. Slevin."

"Agent Alford – Thea – no offence, but how old are you?"

"29"

"So, what I'm hearing is that you believe it's a virus; but it's unlike any other virus you've seen in your 29 years? Is that right?" Slevin asked with a slight edge in his voice that caused Molly's back to stiffen.

Sensing growing tension, Thea quickly responded. "Mr. Slevin what inflicted the sailors had a critical quality that only viruses have."

"Oh? Tell me."

"Dormancy."

"Dormancy?"

"Yes sir, let me explain. If I somehow got you to ingest, or I injected you with, a toxin, your body would react immediately. Strychnine, for example. I inject you with strychnine you start showing symptoms immediately. Even with organic toxins like ptomaine, once you're infected there's a gestation period. But, you're 50+ years old, probably 200 pounds, six plus feet tall. I'm 29, 5'8" and about 115 pounds. My ptomaine gestation period would be much different than yours. If you and I were infected at the exact same time, I would probably start showing symptoms in 5 to 6 hours. In your case, it might be 10 to 12 hours.

"So, what I am saying is that 265lb, 40 year old Master Chief Petty Officer Maguire would have reacted much slower than the helmsman, Petty Officer Marie Ricchio, at, maybe, 105 pounds, 5'5", and 19 years of age. They definitely would not have reacted simultaneously.

"So, dormancy is the telltale characteristic of a virus that leads me to believe that it is, indeed, a virus – of some kind – that we are dealing with here. What we've never seen is a virus that comes alive in all of its host bodies at exactly the same time."

"Admiral, if I may?" Slevin said looking at Molly who nodded.

"We have a unique virus. One that produces its symptoms simultaneously, regardless of body profile. We have a secure naval vessel. One with a 24hr a-day watch. Yet, somehow this unique, exotic virus managed to get on board and infect every member of the crew. I presume there are very carefully kept records of who was allowed aboard as the ship visited these foreign ports. I will also bet that those records tell us absolutely nothing.

"I think we need to assume, as Admiral McNamara has all along, that this isn't just a random string of murders. On the contrary, it has the well-organized markings of a major terrorist group or, I hesitate to say, a hostile foreign power.

"Ladies and gentlemen, I'd say we have our work cut out for us. We have to find out who poisoned our guys and then we have to catch them and bring them to some kind of justice.

"Mr. Slevin, if I may?" Thea spoke up.

"Sir, I think we better find out what killed our guys too. And how it works. So, no one else can use it against us."

"Amen to that." Slevin said to nods around the room.

"Well, bearing all of this in mind, let's get to work.

"May I make a series of suggestions?" Slevin said, looking specifically at Gary and Molly, who both nodded.

"There is a lot of work to do here. So, I suggest that we divide it up between us at the FBI and Tim's people at NCIS. In general, Michael's people should focus, with Thea's help, on looking for the 'what'.

"Thea, if you were looking for research on exotic viruses, where would you go?"

"Fort Detrick, sir."

"Isn't that what you said a couple hours ago, Michael?"

"Exactly." Michael said nodding.

"Good, so both of you start out singing from the same songbook.

"Tim, why don't your people focus on the 'who'? Find the bastards who did this to us. Find the bastards that murdered our guys. That work for you?"

"Good. Now, third. Since we at the FBI have more resources than our brethren at NCIS, why don't we set up a command center at our shop to which all are welcome at all times. Our office is your office. 'Mi casa, tu casa.' That includes you Admiral McNamara. I assume you will want to assign some of your personnel to this case. They gotta have a place to sit. No better place to sit than in the command center right in the middle of the action. And I hesitate to add that wherever your people can contribute to this effort, please tell them to speak up. Does that work for you too, Alison?"

"Fine with me." Alison said.

Slevin looked around the room. He didn't see wild approbation in any of the faces; but he didn't see any objections either.

"Ok, then let's make it happen." Slevin said, after which people began to make motions to get up.

"Uh, ladies and gentlemen, there's one more act in this play." Gary said. And as he said this, the far door opened and the President of the United States walked in with a smile on her face. (When he sensed the meeting was coming to an end, Gary had pushed the 'POTUS' button under the table three times. It was his signal to the President that it was time for her to make her entrance. And the three buzzes signaled the President that all had gone well with the meeting. Hence the smile as she entered.)

"Let's see." The President said moving toward her chair, I know everyone here except this gentleman and this young lady." She said stopping in front of Tim Swift. "You are Mr. Swift of our NCIS, I take it."

"Yes ma'am, nice to meet you."

"And this is?" The President said turning to Thea.

"Ma'am, I am NCIS Special Agent Elisabeth Alford."

"Nice to meet you Agent Alford, welcome to the White House.

"I understand you have had a productive meeting." The President said looking at Gary who nodded.

"Congratulations. I know you all understand what a wild and unique situation we are dealing with here. And I am so pleased that you have all agreed to work together to find out what happened and to catch those who perpetrated these atrocities. It's times like these that we need the utmost cooperation. So, again, I thank you. And good luck." With that, the President headed for the door.

"Mike." Slevin said to Michael Cornell as everyone else began to head for the door. "When you get back to our shop get with Jim Griffin to get this command center set up asap, ok?"

"Right, sir." Michael ended with.

CHAPTER **16**

THE ELEPHANT & CASTLE

At a quarter to seven, Tim Swift was getting out of his car in the parking lot of the Russell-Knox Building in Quantico, Virginia, the headquarters of the Naval Criminal Investigative Service (NCIS), when his cellphone rang. He looked at the caller ID and saw the name "Michael Cornell". He and Michael had exchanged cellphone numbers after the meeting in the Cabinet Room of the White House the previous day.

"You're off to an early start, Agent Cornell." He said into the phone.

"It's not me. Our guys woke me up asking questions about this 'command center' Slevin wants us to create. They've got a lot done already. That's the reason I'm waking you up."

"Not quite waking me up." Swift laughed into the phone. "What do you need?"

"I'd like you to come up as soon as you can to check out the facilities. See if they're going to work for you and your people?"

"I can get up there today. I was actually planning on going to DC today. I've got some other things to take care of up there. What time is good for you?"

"Well, if you can make it around 11:30 or so, we can check out the command center and then go get something to eat across the street. I think we've got a lot of stuff to talk about before getting started with this matter." Michael said.

"I agree." Swift added.

"Oh, and by the way, the official name for what we're doing is the "LRV Project". "LRV" for "Little Rock Virus". That's what we're calling it. The LRV Project and the LRV Command Center.

"Oh, and please come to the 9th and E Streets entrance. I'll have your credentials there."

"K. See you around 11:30." *Slevin is right.* Tim thought. *Cornell IS easy to get along with.*

❈ ❈ ❈ ❈ ❈

The indomitable (and legendary) Jim Griffin had mustered the FBI logistics gurus within minutes of getting the call from Jim Slevin after the White House meeting. He had the staff commandeer two large conference rooms on the sixth floor just down the hall from Slevin's office. Part of the rooms they set up theater-style, for briefings. The rest of the space they organized into cubicles with room dividers. They left several sturdy tables along the inside wall for communications gear that would soon arrive.

Tim Swift nodded approvingly as he walked through the rooms. He greeted several FBI staff who were already moving in.

"I told them to save some of the desks with good views for your people." Michael quipped, gesturing to emphasize the total absence of windows. Swift laughed. "You don't really need to do that. I don't want my people daydreaming. I don't want them looking out the windows all day." Michael laughed softly too. "Speaking of people. How many are you thinking about putting here?"

"Not too many." Tim said. "Just enough to keep your people informed about what we're doing and to keep abreast of what you're doing. And, speaking about what our people are going to be doing, we need to talk about that."

"Agreed. Let's go get some lunch and talk about it." Michael said gesturing to the elevators.

A few minutes later they were sitting down at the table furthest from the entrance and nearest the windows at the Elephant & Castle, 12th & Pennsylvania Avenues.

"I trust you drink beer, good English beer, that is." Michael said.

"Is the bear catholic?" Tim responded.

"Come again?" Michael said.

"Have you not heard the two famous rhetorical questions: 'Does the bear shit in the woods? Is the Pope catholic?'"

"Yes."

"Well, I just switch them around." Tim said with a grin.

It took Michael a second, but when he got it, he laughed out loud. Meanwhile Tim had gone to the bar to inspect the labels on the impressive row of draft choices.

"London Pride." Tim said to the waiter. "ESB (Extra Special Bitter), for me." Michael added.

"Ok." Tim said when the waiter was out of earshot. "How are we going to catch these bastards?"

"Well, first, are you ok with the division of labor that the National Security Advisor was talking about: NCIS focuses on the who and the why. And we focus on the how – or the what - and the why?" Michael asked.

"Sure." Tim said. "Makes perfect sense. I've only got 2500 people but they are everywhere the Navy is. That includes Asia. And, other than Thea Alford and a couple of Thea-wannabes, we're pretty light on the sophisticated scientific talent that you have."

"Well I think that my people and, probably, Thea too will all be taking lessons from the folks at Fort Detrick." Michael added. And then, looking out the window to the ever-heavy traffic on Pennsylvania Avenue, he spoke – almost as if he were talking to himself.

"Why the Navy? Why kill sailors? Why a relatively small ship like an LCV rather that a carrier or a missile cruiser? If you want to make a point, why not kill several hundred – or several thousand – sailors? How did they get the virus on board? Why, and how, did the virus go active all of a sudden? How were all of the sailors - from the slimmest girl to the biggest dude – all affected at exactly the same time. Like on a signal."

When Michael said "signal", Tim's head jerked up and he looked Michael straight in the eye. "Signal." Tim repeated. "That's what I've been thinking too. I even asked Thea."

"What'd she say?"

"Said she'd never heard of a virus that wasn't affected by the age and size of its host organism. She also said she'd never heard of a virus being activated by some sort of signal. But then she said it might be possible."

"Tim, can you get your people out to the last ports that the *Little Rock* put in at?"

"Already underway. I thought we should start wherever the *Little Rock* had ever been."

"Great. But, Tim, aren't visitors on ships – especially in foreign ports – tightly controlled. Shouldn't there be a record of every non-crew member that went aboard the *Little Rock*?"

"There should be. And there is. But nada." Swift said holding his empty palms up. "Since the *Little Rock* began her mission in Norfolk, the only non-crew who boarded the *Little Rock* were a half dozen local dignitaries and 3 of their security people on the tiny island of Mauritius. They attended a reception on the *Little Rock* the day before the virus outbreak."

"Really?"

"Yep. I was planning on sending a couple agents out to Mauritius to check that situation out, but I wanted to talk to you first."

"Do it, man. If that's the only place the *Little Rock* put in, then Mauritius is square one. And, Tim, ask your people to check out all the foreign visitors to Mauritius in the last several weeks.

"What?"

"Have them check out ALL of the foreign visitors to Mauritius."

"Why? What are you thinking?

"I'm thinking that the odds are pretty close to zero that one of the local VIPs who attended the reception on the *Little Rock*, or one of their security guys, are bad guys with a grudge against the U.S. Navy. I'm thinking it's someone else.

"Yeah. I agree. But who? We've got complete records and, as I said, no one other than the VIPs and their security people got aboard the *Little Rock*."

"Tim, I hear you and I agree. But somebody – some body - got the virus on board. We certainly don't know how they did it. But I am thinking that whoever this mystery man was, he was NOT a longtime resident and citizen of Mauritius. I'll bet he was some foreigner who got wind of the *Little Rock's* movements and went to Mauritius specifically to kill those sailors."

"Ok, what do you want us to do?"

"Get with the Mauritian border people. They'll have records of all foreigners who entered the country. Have your people get their list. Then check out everyone on the list. Somebody, or some bodies, on that list are bad guys. For sure."

"Will do." Tim Swift said.

"How about the ship itself?"

"What. What do you mean, 'the ship itself'?

"You know. The ship. The superstructure. The hull. The ship."

"Did anyone go over the structure of the ship to see if there were any signs of tampering or introducing any foreign substances.

"I don't know. I don't think Thea did. That's really a Navy thing. My people wouldn't know what to look for." Tim said.

"Speaking of the Navy, I wonder who Admiral McNamara is sending to work with us? Michael said.

"I figured you'd know if anyone knew." Swift said smiling.

Just then a Naval officer's uniform appeared at the door and Michael saw the hostess point in his and Swift's direction. A woman lieutenant commander walked resolutely down the aisle towards them. When she got to their table, she stopped and asked "Agent Michael Cornell?"

"Yep. How do you know that?" Michael asked squinting.

"Your office said you were at lunch and a friend of yours told me where you liked to eat." She then came to attention, saluted and said: "Lieutenant Commander Breanna Sisk reporting for duty, sir."

"Are you our gift from Admiral McNamara, Commander?" Michael said smiling broadly.

"I'm one of them, sir. I am the Special Ops Officer assigned to the CNO's office. But, I'm sure the Admiral will send more than just me."

"Well, you're a good start, Commander." Michael said, again smiling.

"By the way, sir, people call me Brea." Pause. "I hear tell you go by Michael."

"That I do, Brea. And…." Michael said as he pulled up a chair for her. "as your seafaring colleagues would say: 'welcome aboard'", gesturing for Brea to sit.

As she sat down in the chair next to Michael, she looked across the table and said: "And I'll bet you're Tim Swift."

"How did you know?" He said.

"I'm clairvoyant." Brea said.

"Yes, but why so formal, calling me Tim? Why not call me Tootsie?"

"I know you're kidding. But don't you go by Tim, or do I call you 'Director'?"

"Just kidding, Brea. We should all be friends. 'Tim' is fine."

"How did you get the name 'Tim'? I read that your full name was Harlan Justin Swift, junior."

"You don't want to know, Brea. It's a long story. I'll tell you another time.

"Brea, first, do you want lunch?" Michael interjected.

"No, I'm good. Thank you anyway."

"Well then, down to business. Tim and I were just talking about a Naval assignment when you came in. As you know, we don't know how this virus got on board. So, Tim's people are going to Mauritius, the *Little Rock's* only port-of-call, not only to check out the locals who got on board, but also any foreigners who were on the island when the *Little Rock* was there. But, since the only people who got on board were local dignitaries and their security people, we don't have much hope there. And absolutely no other foreigners got aboard. So, we're thinking how could the virus get on board. And we're thinking there might be some sort of device, or piece of equipment, that somehow introduced the virus.

"As you can tell, we're shooting in the dark here, but we have nothing else to go on. So, can you get your people to go over the entire ship with a microscope looking for anything – absolutely anything – out of the ordinary. We're hoping that if there was a device of some kind that there might be some remnant or trace of it still onboard."

"Consider it done." Brea said looking up from the notes she was taking. "What about the crew? What if one of those sailors was a suicidal maniac?"

"That's what my people are working on too, Brea." Tim said. "We're going over each of those sailor's backgrounds with the proverbial microscope."

"Ok." Brea said slowly and sat there tapping her pen on the notepad.

After a minute, Tim said with a smile: "Anything wrong, Commander?"

"Thea Alford works for you, doesn't she Tim?"

"Yes, why?"

"I'm thinking that if I want this done right, I'm going to have to go out to Diego Garcia myself and supervise this operation. And since I have no clue what we could possibly be looking for, I thought if would be good if Thea went with me. She may not know much, but she certainly knows more than I do."

"Good idea." Tim said. "Why don't you talk to her and tell her I agree that she should go."

"Will do." Brea said, putting away her pen and notepad.

✷ ✷ ✷ ✷ ✷

Four days later, Michael and Molly McNamara were on her yacht in Baltimore harbor getting dressed for dinner ashore at The Boathouse, when his phone rang. It was Brea calling from Diego Garcia.

"Sorry to bother you on a weekend, Michael, but something important has come up."

"No problem, Brea. What's up?"

"Well we put together a good detail who literally went over every square inch of the ship with a fine tooth comb. Even Thea was impressed. But they found nothing. Nada. Zip.

"Now Thea says that we need to inspect the bottom of the ship. The hull, that's underwater, of course.

"That's going to be a major operation. Several divers working long hours. It's going to take me a while to organize it, if we have to do it. So, that's why I am calling. Do we have to inspect the hull?"

"Brea, I hate to spoil your day, but I think the answer is yes."

"I was afraid you were going to say that. Ok, I'm on it."

✷ ✷ ✷ ✷ ✷

The following evening Michael and Molly were back in DC having a glass of wine on Michael's deck before going out for dinner in Georgetown, when his phone rang again. Brea again.

"Don't tell me you got results this fast. I didn't expect to hear from you for several days."

"Bingo, Michael. We found it! We found the device they used to get the virus on board!

"You did? That's terrific! What the hell is it?"

"It's like a mesh bag that was affixed to the hull over the drinking water intake. It was stuck on with some kind of adhesive. Looks like a very professional job. Thea says that whenever the crew opened the water intake to desalinate seawater that the virus went aboard with the water. That's how it infected the crew."

"Wow! That's incredible. Have you told Swift yet?"

"No. It was you that wanted the ship searched."

"Ok. But he's got to know. So, he can call his people off checking out the crew's backgrounds. Do you want to call him, or should I?"

"You call him, Michael. I'm exhausted."

"Ok. You and Thea get some rest. Then, let me know when you're getting back."

"I want to get you and Thea to get with Tim and me and the rest of the team for a complete debrief. Ok?"

"Ok."

"Safe travels."

CHAPTER **17**

DER BUNDESNACHRICHTENDIENST

"Jake, what are you doing here at this hour?" Michael said to John Jekielek, the new #3 man at the FBI as he walked into the Command Center. When former President Bill Richardson had promoted Jim Slevin to head the Bureau, Jim had promoted Jake to his old job as Executive Assistant Director for the National Security Branch. But there was one small hitch, as Jim explained to Jake: Michael Cornell's Environmental and Biological Operations Office (EBOO) would report to Jekielek only on paper. In reality, EBOO would report directly to Slevin. Jake readily agreed. So, Jake was Michael's boss on paper; but not really. And, besides, they were good friends.

It was only a little after 6am. Michael always got in early. Jake seldom did.

"My guys told me there was some big news coming in from the NCIS people in Mauritius." Jake said handing a couple sheets of paper to Michael. Michael looked the pages over. "Well, I guess so!" Michael said raising his eyebrows.

The NCIS agents had reported that Mauritian Border Police told them that two German nationals had entered Mauritius two days before the *Little Rock*. The FBI had determined that the names on their passports were false. Furthermore, the following day, two Korean visitors entered Mauritius. The FBI determined these two men had false passports too. Finally, two days before the *Little Rock*, a mysterious Turkish national with a German passport entered Mauritius. It turned out that this Turk was a professor at Ludwigs Maximillian University in Munich. His name was Mustafa al-Khalid.

It seems that Mauritius doesn't get many Korean visitors. The border police were suspicious. They thought the two men definitely didn't look like tourists, yet they had tourist visas. So they had photocopied their passports including fingerprints and pictures. The NCIS agents had obtained copies and would be faxing them in a few hours from the U.S. Embassy there. Mustafa al-Khalid and the two Germans also had tourist visas.

"We're getting this info to the Navy, too, aren't we?" Michael asked.

"For sure." Jake said.

"Does Swift know?" Michael asked addressing one of the NCIS agents seconded to the Command Center. "Yes, sir. He does now."

"OK, we should be able to deal with the prints and the mug shots in a few hours, no?" Michael asked to a chorus of yes-nods.

"Please ask Swift if he can make a meeting here this afternoon. Also ask Brea if she can get together this afternoon." Michael said to the young Lieutenant, who was part of the Navy team. "Or if not, please ask Admiral McNamara to send us another of her senior people. This could be the break we've been looking for." Again, a room full of nodding heads.

❊ ❊ ❊ ❊ ❊

A couple hours later Michael's cellphone signaled he was getting a text message. It was from Molly McNamara. It said: "Please call me from SCIF." A "SCIF" is a "Sensitive Compartmented Information Facility". A lot of silly military words to describe a safe room where secret matters could be discussed. Michael walked down the hall to the SCIF on the sixth floor and dialed Molly's official number at the Pentagon on the secure telephone. It was answered by a Chief in Molly's office but he put Michael directly through to the Admiral.

"Hello, little friend. What's up?" Michael said.

"This shithead, Mustafa al-Khalid, the Turkish professor at the university in Munich? We know him."

"Really? How so? What do you know about him?"

"This is so unreal. You're not going to believe it." Molly said. Twelve years ago, this dude proposed marriage to a young woman whose father was the head of the Muslim Brotherhood. We now don't think that Mustafa knew about this. But the Brotherhood had been organizing and financing terrorist attacks on us.

"Mustafa's family are very wealthy. They own the largest brewery in Turkey. Yes, alcohol in a Muslim country! Mustafa decided to celebrate his forthcoming marriage to this girl with a lavish engagement party on his family's 100+ foot yacht off the coast of Kusadasi.

"Well, the girl's father had the bad sense to invite five members of the Brotherhood's ruling council to the party. We of course were listening to all of this. Someone in my operation, or maybe the CIA – I am not sure who it was – ordered an air strike on the party by a Reaper drone. So, the U.S. Navy fired a Hellfire missile at the party boat and, apparently, killed almost everyone on board. Everyone, that is, except Mustafa who spent months in cosmetic surgery getting his face repaired.

"So, by all appearances, Mustafa al-Khalid is this nerdy classics professor at Ludwigs Maximillian University in Munich; but he sure has a big reason to hate and carry a grudge against the United States and our Navy."

"Well, I'll be damned." Was about all that Michael could say. "I guess he sure does."

❊ ❊ ❊ ❊ ❊

A couple hours later, Michael, Tim Swift, Brea and Jake were all in Slevin's office. Michael had felt that Slevin should know what the NCIS had learned and what Admiral McNamara had told him. So he told Selvin. Slevin then wanted to be at this meeting and called it for his own office.

Brea had never met Slevin or Jake. So the meeting began with some courtly salutations and good-natured bantering.

The meeting officially began with Swift reiterating what his people had learned in Mauritius. Then Jake chimed in about what the FBI knew about the passports. Then he dropped a bombshell on the meeting.

"Folks, we just learned something important a few minutes ago. First, the fingerprints of the two Koreans belong to two commanders in the North Korean Navy."

"Holy shit!" Slevin said for everyone.

"One of them, named Ri Sang Soo is assigned to the North Korean Embassy in Berlin. The other guy, Ryu Dae Hee, is regular Navy from Pyongyang. Curiously, he's involved in vessel construction. He's some kind of expert in shipbuilding.

"Well, that certainly fits with what we know about how the virus got on board the *Little Rock*." Brea interjected. "He certainly must know about water intakes."

"Wait! There's more." Jake said.

The two Germans had told the Mauritian border police that their employer was the *Stiftung Erdlust*, at the mention of which both Michael and Slevin straightened up in their chairs.

"Those bastards!" Slevin said.

"Yes." Jake said. "Those bastards!"

"What's the *Stiftung Erdlust*?" Said Swift. "Yeah, what's that?" Said Brea.

"They are a non-profit scientific think tank, located in Munich, that hire themselves out to do brain work for terrorist organizations." Slevin said.

"Speaking about "hiring themselves out" and speaking about Munich, Brea why don't you tell us what the Navy knows about the last visitor to Mauritius that we're looking at." Michael said.

"Yes, that's right. Both Munich and the money to buy the *Stiftung Erdlust* people. That would be our other suspect, Mustafa al-Khalid." So, Brea told them the same story that Admiral McNamara had told both Michael and her.

"Well, it certainly looks like we've got a German connection here." Slevin said. "We've got two scientific rent-a-brains from Munich in the company of a Turkish professor from Munich, who ostensibly hates the United States, and certainly her Navy, and has more money than God. And we've got a North Korean naval attaché, stationed in Germany, in the company of a man with the knowledge of how the virus got aboard the *Little Rock*. And they all just happen to wind up together on the little island of Mauritius just before the *Little Rock* is poisoned. What a coincidence!

"So, what do we do now?" Slevin asked, looking around the room.

Jake and Michael looked at each other for a second and Michael nodded.

"Jim." Jake said. "We think we need to bring in the Germans."

There was a several second pause. Then Slevin said: "I was afraid you didn't invite me to this meeting because of my good looks." Everyone smiled wanly.

"I think you all know that I can't authorize this myself. I'll have to bring in the White House." And then, after another brief pause. "And so I will do just that."

"What part of Germany are we talking about here?" Slevin asked.

"The *Bundesnachrichtendienst*." Michael answered

"The BND, hunh? That's what I thought. Well, it'll be convenient for them. They're headquartered right there in Munich too."

"The *Bundesnachrichtendienst*, hunh?" Slevin mused looking out the window. I've always thought that's sure a big mouthful of words."

"Well, 'the Federal Bureau of Investigation' is not exactly a three-letter word either." Michael chimed in.

"Yes, but *Bundesnachrichtendienst* is just one word. Anyway, boys and girl." Slevin said nodding nicely at Brea. "I shall go to the White House and get back to all of you. Thank you all very much."

CHAPTER **18**

CONFESSIONS

Most of Mustafa's and Nicola's conversations the first few days of his stay centered around their years together at Le Rosey and the times they managed to get together during their respective university careers.

No fool, Mustafa. During these days he also had Nicola's story checked out in Switzerland. His money manager in London, Lindsay Grace, had all sorts of connections on the dark side of the law in many countries. Mustafa found out the truth. About the dead patients and the missing money.

Several days later Mustafa and Nicola were enjoying beers at Mustafa's favorite table in the Hofbräuhaus, Munich's enormous, legendary, state-owned beer hall.

"You know that picture on my mantle?" Mustafa asked.

"You mean the one of you and Jasmine?"

"Yes. I need to tell you about that."

"Are you sure you want to talk about it?" Nicola said. He knew that Jasmine had died in an explosion on Mustafa's yacht during their engagement party. The same explosion that had maimed Mustafa. Nicola assumed that the memories were very painful for his friend.

"Yes. You see. You don't know the entire story. And I want you to know it."

Mustafa then told Nicola that Jasmine's father was the head

of the Muslim Brotherhood. At the time, no one knew this: neither Mustafa nor even Jasmine. No one, that is, except U.S. Intelligence. It turns out that Jasmine's father had invited several of the high council of the Brotherhood to the engagement party. Apparently U.S. Intelligence knew this too. Because there was no ordinary explosion. No, Mustafa's boat was attacked by the United States Navy. They fired a missile from a drone. That is how Jasmine and everyone else were killed. Mustafa could see the look of disbelief on Nicola's face.

"That is the absolute truth my friend. I would never speak falsely about a matter such as that."

"Of course." Nicola said in a low voice.

"Now, that is not the end to the story. Every time I look at that photograph I think of Jasmine. But I also think about the United States Navy. So, now I will tell you chapter 2 of the story."

Mustafa then told Nicola about finding a German foundation that specialized in certain scientific research. "You might call it 'black science'". Mustafa said. He told about paying them to develop a virus, which he called the Calypso Virus. "Kaluptein" in Greek means "to hide". The effects of the virus were hidden – hidden, that is, until the virus was activated. He then told about infecting the entire crew of a small U.S. warship in the Indian Ocean. Mustafa told Nicola that when his people activated the virus all of the sailors murdered each other. Nicola's eyes were wide in astonishment and his eyebrows were raised almost off his forehead.

When Nicola regained a modicum of composure, Mustafa said to him. "Now that I have told you who I am, I want you to tell me who you are." The astonished face returned to Nicola.

"I want you to tell me about Switzerland. I know what happened, my friend; but I want to hear it in your own words. And don't be afraid. At the end of your story we will still be best friends."

Nicola turned bright red and looked around, squirming in his seat. But he could see a genuine look of kindness in Mustafa's face. So he told Mustafa the full story. He told him about the Swiss magistrate's ultimatum – jail or leave Switzerland. "So that, you see, is why I am here." He ended.

"And, I am, indeed, glad that you are here." Mustafa said kindly.

"What do you propose to do here in Munich?" Mustafa asked.

"Medicine." Nicola said. "My Swiss license is valid here."

"Yes, but medicine is tightly controlled by the state here, as it is in Switzerland. Not much money in it. State salaries." Mustafa said.

"Well, then I'll just have to find a way to make some additional money." Nicola said with a straight face. Neither man flinched. But they both knew what Nicola meant.

"Fine." Mustafa added. "I would like to bring you together with a colleague and business partner, Herr Doktor Horst Maier. Dr. Maier is the head of the *Stiftung Erdlust*. It is an organization that does science for people like me. They developed the virus that we used on the U.S. Navy. I need to have a very important conversation with him. But I want you to meet him because he can probably bring you many medical patients who need your help."

❖ ❖ ❖ ❖ ❖

Three days later Mustafa, Nicola and Dr. Maier were sitting at the same table in the Hofbraühaus. The hall was filled with tourists. Very noisy. Just the way Mustafa liked it. Less chance of his conversation being overheard.

Mustafa introduced Nicola and Dr. Maier. He told Dr. Maier that Nicola would be starting up a medical practice in gerontology. He asked Dr. Maier to help find patients for him.

"I will be most happy to do so." Dr. Maier said.

Mustafa then turned toward Dr. Maier and said that he had told Nicola about the Calypso Virus.

"You did?" Said Dr. Maier, shocked. "I thought we explicitly agreed that that matter would stay between you and me only."

"Dear Dr. Maier." Mustafa said kindly. "Now, when you think of me, you must think of both Nicola and me. We are best friends. What I know, he will know. When you speak to me, you are speaking to him too. And vice versa. Do you understand?"

"Yes, Herr Professor Doktor." Dr. Maier said rather stiffly, using Mustafa's academic title.

"Good." Mustafa said with finality. "Now I need to tell you both where we are going from here.

"Dr. Maier." Mustafa began. "We are going to need much more of your virus. Our next target won't be a small boat full of American sailors. Our next target will be the largest surface water system in the world." Mustafa looked at the faces of both men.

"My friends, we are going to inject the Calypso Virus into the water of the City of New York in the United States."

"The City of New York?" Both Nicola and Dr. Maier said equally in disbelief.

"There are 8 million people in the City of New York! You want to poison 8 million people?" Dr. Maier said, again, in shock.

"Yes, I do." Mustafa said coldly.

"Eight million people. Lieber Gott." Dr. Maier said softly staring off into space.

CHAPTER **19**

LONDON CALLING

Mustafa was in a foul mood after the meeting with Dr. Maier where he disclosed his plan to attack New York City. He went to his room as soon as he and Nicola got home. He always told the *Dienstfrau* to have breakfast ready promptly at 8am. The next morning Nicola sat at the table until 10am, when Mustafa emerged looking drawn. He complained of difficulty sleeping and of a severe headache. Nicola was very solicitous. He asked Mustafa several questions about his symptoms and then said: "My friend, I have some Depakene in my medical bag. It is for severe headaches like the one you have. I have headaches sometimes. I take it too." Nicola lied. He knew he was lying about taking Depakene himself, but it was a white lie; he thought it would make Mustafa more comfortable to know that Nicola took the same drug. It worked. Mustafa took the 2 Depakene tablets Nicola offered. He then made a cold compress and lay down on a couch with the compress on his forehead.

Mustafa lay still and drifted in and out of sleep until after 1pm. He then rose and found Nicola reading in his bedroom. He suggested lunch at the Chinese Tower Beer Garden nearby in the English Garden, the huge park in the center of Munich, which was close to their apartment.

"I was very upset with Herr Doktor Maier's reaction to my plan."

Mustafa said using the unnecessarily formal title for Maier to express his displeasure with the Doktor.

"I could see that." Nicola said. "But I was actually quite taken by surprise too."

"I realize that." Mustafa said gently. "This little terror game – or, as I think of it, counter terror game – is very new to you. I expect you will get used to it. You are not new to what we are doing. We are just doing it on a much bigger scale."

Nicola blushed. The phrase Mustafa used "You are not new to what we are doing." meant that Nicola was not new to murdering people.

"But Maier is another story. He has been in on this since the beginning. He knew we were going to use the Calypso Virus on human beings. American human beings! And American human beings serving in their Navy to be absolutely precise! So, this should not have come as a shock to him. Mustafa was starting to get heated. Nicola reached out for Mustafa's arm. Mustafa looked down at Nicola's hand and said: "Yes, you are right, of course. I shouldn't let this upset me."

"Nicola, I have given Dr. Maier millions of dollars to develop the Calypso Virus. He will make more of it for me so that I can carry out my plans against the Americans. That I can assure you. But I will need to stay on top of him, so to speak. I will have to work more closely with him to see that enough virus is prepared.

"Now, Nicola, you are probably wondering how you fit it to this Calypso Virus business. The answer is that you don't. I don't want you to get personally involved in this business of mine with Maier. But I do want you to know what I am doing. I want to be able to talk to you about my plans and what we are doing to make them real."

Nicola nodded. "You know whenever you need me I am here."

Mustafa nodded gently. "But you will be a busy man in the next few weeks." Mustafa went on to tell Nicola that he was setting up a monthly payment of €50,000 for him to help him get started with his medical practice. Nicola needed to open up a bank account right away. And, Mustafa went on: an apartment below in the same building was coming vacant and for sale. Mustafa said he was going to buy it and put it in Nicola's name. Finally, he said that Nicola would be busy picking out furniture for the new apartment, and that "his people" would make arrangements for paying for all of it.

The following day, as Mustafa instructed him, Nicola took €500 and went to the Bayerische Landesbank, or BayernLB, and opened an account. The Bayern LB was majority owned by the State of Baveria, and was one of the largest banks in Germany. Nicola dutifully opened the account and set up all the codes and passwords so he could bank online and use the, *Geldautomat*, or ATM. Two days later Nicola checked his account balance and saw that a deposit of €50,000 had been made the day before.

Mustafa bought the vacant apartment on the third floor it and put it in Nicola's name, as promised. The apartment was unfurnished. Mustafa told Nicola to pick out furniture and order it and tell Mustafa how much it would all cost. Mustafa would have the funds deposited into Nicola's account. And so Nicola spent more time than he wanted to looking for furniture – furniture that would meet Mustafa's approval.

Mustafa went to work with Dr. Maier 3 days a week. Each day he told the *Dienstfrau* to prepare dinner. After his sessions with Dr. Maier, Mustafa didn't feel like dining out. More and more he was coming home with migraine headaches, which Nicola treated with the Depakene. One day Nicola gave Mustafa a written prescription for the Depakene. 40 pills. One a day for Mustafa for the next month and 10 to replenish Nicola's medical bag. Nicola wanted Mustafa to have the opportunity to talk to a pharmacist about the Depakene. Mustafa knew that Nicola had murdered several patients with drugs. He wanted to allay any suspicions that Mustafa might have about the Depakene.

One night while dining at home, Nicola got up and went to the kitchen for a bottle of beer. When he got there he heard a loud crash in the dining room. He immediately ran back. He saw Mustafa writhing on the floor with a broken wine glass in his hand. Nicola went to him. Examined Mustafa's eyes and checked his mouth for any choking. Then he ran to his room and took a vial of Topiramate and a syringe and went back to Mustafa and injected him. Nicola covered Mustafa with a blanket and sat next to him on the floor. Within minutes Nicola, saw the drug beginning to take effect. Fifteen minutes later Mustafa was fine and began talking.

"I don't know what happened. My headache was not going away this time and I reached for my glass of wine and that's all I remember. What happened?"

"You had a seizure."

"A seizure, dear God!"

"No, no. It's not as bad as you might think. Seizures and migraines are physiological cousins. Only seizures are the evil cousin. I gave you a shot of a drug called Topiramate. It's for seizures but can also be used for extremely severe migraines. Nicola held up the empty vial so Mustafa could read the name of the drug. He wanted Mustafa to be able to quiz his pharmacist about the Topiramate too.

As time went on, Mustafa was more and more unpleasant. He came home at dinnertime. Never wanted to eat out any more. He complained bitterly about Dr. Maier, who seemed to be making little progress manufacturing the amount of virus Mustafa wanted. He was having migraines almost every and had had two more seizures. Nicola, had to medicate him daily.

One afternoon, Nicola went out in the English Garden for a run. When he got back he picked up his phone and noticed there was a voicemail. Odd. Nicola didn't get many calls now that he moved to Germany. It was from London. A woman named Lindsay Grace, who apparently managed at least some of Mustafa's money. She identified herself as an officer of the "Hilton Bank". Lindsay left a voice message saying that Nicola would need to come to London to sign some papers for Mustafa's account.

At dinner, Nicola asked Mustafa about the call from London.

"Oh, yes, Miss Grace. A very nice and very smart young woman. You should make plans to go to London. She needs you to sign some papers regarding your new apartment. I'm sure she'll treat you like a king."

So, Nicola returned Lindsay's call the next day and made plans to fly to London in 2 weeks. Lindsay said she would take care of the flights and have a car and a driver meet Nicola at the airport.

A couple days later Nicola returned from a run in the English

Garden to find another voice message on his phone. He assumed it was Lindsay calling with details about his trip, so he didn't look at it till later. When he did, he realized it wasn't from Lindsay's number. No, the prefix indicated the caller was right there in Munich. The problem was that Nicola didn't know anyone in Munich other than Mustafa.......and, of course, Herr Doktor Horst Maier. So, Nicola listened to the voice message. It was Dr. Maier. He addressed Nicola as "Dr. Angelini". The message said that he needed to talk to Nicola – alone. Dr. Maier specified "alone" three times in the brief message. He asked Nicola to return his call at 2pm the following day. That suited Nicola fine. 2pm was the time he liked to run in the English Garden. He'd be able to make the call in total privacy.

Nicola knew from Mustafa's worsening health that matters were not going well at all with Dr. Maier. So, he was very interested in what Dr. Maier had to say.

"Maier hier." The voice said into the phone. "Dr. Maier, it's Nicola Angelini calling as you requested."

"Yes, thank you for calling, Dr. Angelini. Dr. Angelini we need to talk about our mutual friend, Mustafa."

"I thought so, Dr. Maier. What do you have in mind?"

"Mustafa tells me that you like to run in the English Garden this time of day. I, too, like either to take a walk or go to the gym after lunch. So, I thought we might each skip our exercise and meet at the Wirtshaus Ayingers. Do you know Ayingers? It's right across the *Platzl* from the Hofbraühaus where we met the first time?"

"I'll find it." Nicola said. "When?"

"Tomorrow at this time, if that suits you Dr. Angelini?"

"That would be fine. I'll see you then."

❊ ❊ ❊ ❊ ❊

"Doktor Angelini, so good of you to come." Dr. Maier said pronouncing "Angelini" with the hard German "g" instead of the soft Italian one.

"Dr. Angelini, I believe our friend is losing his mind. He does not believe facts I report to him."

"I'm sorry, Dr. Maier. I don't follow you. What facts?"

"Doktor Angelini, there are two major reasons why we cannot manufacture enough virus for Mustafa's plan for New York City. Let me tell you, the New York City water system consumes over 4.5 billion cubic meters of water a day. That is 4.5 million liters of water. For the virus to act, we would need a 0.1% solution. That, Doktor Angelini, means we would have to produce some 4.5 million liters of the virus. That would be about 4,500 cubic meters of virus. The typical tank truck holds about 30 cubic meters of fluid. That would mean that we would need a fleet of 150 tank trucks to deliver the virus to the reservoirs in New York. Doktor Angelini, I ask you, does anyone in his right mind think we could put 150 truck loads of virus into the New York City water system without getting arrested by every law enforcement agency in the region?

"Furthermore." Dr. Maier added before Nicola could say anything. "The critical enzyme needed to grow the virus would be needed in quantities of about 10% of the quantity of the virus itself. In other words, we would need 15 truckloads of the enzyme to grow the virus.

"The last straw, Doktor Angelini, is this: do you know where this enzyme is produced? It is produced by the United States Army at a base called Fort Detrick in the State of Maryland! Fort Detrick produces these enzymes in one-liter batches. I had to order the relatively small amount we needed for the *Little Rock* through several major institutions all of whom were delighted to order it from Fort Detrick and sell it to me at a huge profit. But, how, in God's name, does Mustafa think we could get the American Army to make us 15 truck loads?"

CHAPTER **20**

CHARLES, THE BARMAN

The plane to London had been flying north in the afternoon. Nicola had closed the shade on the window next to him on the left side of the plane to keep the sun out of his eyes. But as the pilot announced their final approach and made a 90° turn to the east, he pulled up the shutter and looked out on the green fields west of Heathrow Airport. A car and driver would be waiting for him at Heathrow to take him to Miss Lindsay Grace.

He thought back to his eventful discussion with Dr. Horst Maier. Poisoning New York City wasn't going to happen. But it probably wouldn't have happened anyway, even if they could have grown the virus. He shook his head. A convoy of 150 tank trucks dumping poison into the Croton reservoir. Preposterous! Totally crazy!

Nicola had agreed with Dr. Maier that the New York project was over. Finished. But then Nicola asked what could be done with the virus in small quantities? Dr. Maier was incredulous. "What do you mean?" He almost shouted at Nicola.

"Dr. Maier, I understand that Mustafa pays you very well to produce the virus."

"He does." Dr. Maier agreed.

"I assume that you would like to keep receiving his money?"

"Of course, but how, if we can't make the thousands of cubic meters of the virus that Mustafa wants.

"Dr. Maier." Nicola had told him. "Just start making the virus."

"What about Mustafa? Sooner or later, he'll catch on."

"Leave Mustafa to me, Dr. Maier. Just leave Mustafa to me."

"Oh, Dr. Maier?" Nicola said at the end of their conversation. "How much money do you get from Mustafa each month and where does the money come from? How does he get it to you?"

"Well, if you must know, we receive €250,000 each month from a company in London."

"What company in London? Do you remember?"

"I'm not sure. Some firm. Same name as a hotel chain. I've only spoken with one of their young agents."

"Was the company's name Hilton?"

"Yes, that's it, Hilton."

"And was the young agent's name Grace, by any chance?"

"Yes, that's the name. Sounded like a young girl. Do you know her?"

"She is about to become my best friend." Nicola said cryptically as he stood to leave.

And so as Nicola's plane hit the tarmac at Heathrow, he thought to himself that he and Miss Grace had much to talk about.

❄ ❄ ❄ ❄ ❄

"I'm Dr. Angelini." Nicola said to a large scuffy man in a leather jacket and cap holding up a paper sign with his name on it just outside the gates where passengers were met.

"My name's Bob, Doctor." The man said in his best cockney accent. "I'll be your driver for your stay here in Britain."

And so began a 40-minute drive to central London along the M-4 motorway.

"Miss Grace is putting you up at the Stafford. Nice place, the Stafford. Very posh. It's in St. James'. Very nice location." Bob said as they entered city traffic.

When they arrived at the hotel, Bob handed Nicola his bag and a card with his phone number on it. "St. James is a great place for a walkabout. But if you're going farther than St. James, just give me a call and I'll be here in just a couple of minutes to take you where you want to go."

When Nicola was checking in, the clerk told him that Miss Grace was waiting for him in the bar. A bellman appeared and took Nicola's bag. "If you're going to the bar, sir, would you like me to unpack for you?" The bellman asked.

"No. That's fine. I'll see to it myself. Thank you."

When Nicola entered the bar, there were a few people sitting at the few tables and there was one lone woman sitting at a table in the back near the window. She stood up and held out her hand. She was tall with a lithe, athletic figure, and glossy brown hair that fell just past her shoulders. She was fresh-faced, with a light smattering of freckles, yet dignified looking with clear blue, cat-like eyes.

"Miss Grace?" Nicola said holding out his hand.

"I prefer Lindsay. And may I call you Nicola? Mustafa refers to you as Nicola, never Nick." She said shaking Nicola's hand firmly.

"What will you have to drink?" Lindsay said as the Barman approached.

"What do you recommend? What are you having?"

"Well, I was just having a cup of tea just to pass the time till you got here. Now, it's time for something serious."

"Like what?" Nicola said with a wry smile.

"Like a Martini! Charles makes the best Martinis in the world."

"Really?"

"Yes, and we have it in writing. Come I'll show you. We have to watch Charles make our drinks. It's a new art form."

Lindsay and Nicola got up and walked over to the bar. Charles, the Barman, emerged from the curtain behind the bar with two cocktail glasses fresh from the freezer. Then he went back behind the curtain and emerged with a clear bottle encased in a block of ice. He had a towel around the ice so he could hold it. He poured each of the cocktail glasses almost to the brim. "Vodka." Charles announced. "Stolichnaya. A very special batch of Stolichnaya".

"Now, here's where the artwork comes in." Lindsay said lighting up Charles' face.

Charles pulled a small crystal bottle out from under the bar. It's cap was an eyedropper with a black rubber top. "Miss Grace likes hers wet, sir." Charles said looking at Nicola. "That would mean two drops of Noilly Pratt, sir. Do you like yours wet or dry, sir?" "Dry." Nicola said. "Then that would be one drop sir." At that, Charles squeezed 2 drops of Vermouth into Lindsay's glass and one into his.

"Cheers!" Lindsay said, picking up her glass and clinking it with Nicola's.

"Charles, may I see the article. I'd like to show it to Dr. Angelini."

"Of course, Miss. You know we'll have it up on the wall next week. The nobs are having it framed and mounted." Charles said referring to the hotel management.

"Will you be staying with us, sir?" Charles said to Nicola. "Yes, indeed." Nicola replied. "It's Dr. Angelini, is it? Well, I am Charles and I am at your service, sir." Charles said extending his hand. "Nice to make your acquaintance." Nicola said shaking Charles' hand.

The article was from *The Sunday Times*. Its title was "The Ten Best Martinis in the World". The Stafford was at the top of the list. Charles, the Barman, and his secret recipe were prominently displayed, with picture of Charles with his arms around the block of ice holding the vodka.

"This is just great!" Nicola said to Charles before returning to the window table with Lindsay.

"Ok, Lindsay, my new friend, I understand you've got some pieces of paper for me to sign. And then, I have a matter I'd like to talk to you about."

"Oh, you do, do you? Funny, you should say that. I actually have several matters I need to talk to YOU about. And, if you must know, the paper signing was for Mustafa's benefit. I could just as easily have sent them to a *Rechtsanwalt* in Munich – using the German word for lawyer – and had you sign them there. No, we have some serious matters to discuss." Lindsay said with a big smile.

"Well from the smile on your face, I guess I'm not going to get murdered in my sleep, or am I, Miss Grace?"

"Since we're going to talk tomorrow, you're safe for tonight." Lindsay said laughing out loud.

"Oh, and what are we going to talk about tomorrow?" Nicola asked mischievously.

"Well, let's see. There's you and Mustafa. There's Dr. Maier and

Mustafa. Then there's Lindsay Grace and Mustafa. So, as you see, Mustafa is the common thread for all these conversations. There is one other common thread: money. M-O-N-E-Y" She spelled it out. "So shall we talk at, say, nine tomorrow morning. The hotel will let us talk right here in this room. No other patrons. No Charles. No one else to disturb us or listen in."

"That works for me." Nicola said smiling. ""I like the agenda."

"Oh, one other thing." Lindsay said as she stood up. "Mustafa's seriously ill, isn't he?"

"Yes."

"Are you treating him?"

"Yes."

"With Adrephine?" Lindsay asked using the name of the drug Nicola used to murder his rich patients in Switzerland.

"Well, aren't you the smart little girl?" Nicola said hoping he wasn't visibly blushing.

"Mustafa told me he told you. Whom do you think Mustafa asked to check out your past in Switzerland in the first place?"

"I'm looking at her."

"You guessed it. See you in the morning." Lindsay sang as she walked away.

❄ ❄ ❄ ❄ ❄

Nicola got up. Signed Charles's chit, went to his room, unpacked, sat down on his bed, and looked out the window. At nothing. Tucked into this little corner of St. James, there were no views of anything other than buildings out of any of the Stafford's windows.

Finally he got up. Took a long walk around St. James to Trafalgar and down Whitehall to Westminster and the River. Then back. Into the bar for one more of Charles' martinis and a little interesting banter with Charles. Turns out Lindsay did a good amount of business in the bar at the Stafford but never seemed to join any of her male guests in the rooms upstairs. Then dinner in the hotel. Then early bed.

Next morning. Early breakfast. Another walk to Westminster. Then back to the Stafford for coffee and round two with Lindsay Grace.

"Sleep well?" Lindsay asked as she breezed into the bar empty but for Nicola.

"Like a stone. And you?"

"Same." She said. "Why thank you, how thoughtful." She said sitting down in front of the cup of coffee Nicola had poured for her.

"Since money runs through all of the matters we have to discuss, why don't we begin there?" Lindsay said. Nicola nodded.

"Ok, well, I send Dr. Maier €250,000 each month and I sent you €50,000 to help start up your medical practice. I will also pay for your new apartment and all of the furnishings. Plus, Mustafa said you might need a little more cash to get your practice going. If so, I'll get it to you. So, you see I am definitely Dr. Maier's banker, and I am sort of yours too.

Lindsay then leaned across the table and said very softly: "Dr. Angelini, I have never told another living soul this but Mustafa pays me under the counter far more than he pays my firm for my services."

"Under the counter?" Nicola asked quizzically.

"Off the books. My employer knows nothing about these payments. As you know I officially work for C.A.S. Hilton Bankers. They manage a good deal of Mustafa's money. But I manage more of his money on my own. Nothing to do with Hiltons. And I get paid directly by Mustafa for managing these funds."

"Oh…..ok?" Nicola said, again quizzically.

"So, the matter we need to discuss and the reason for my smart-ass remark about the Adrephine last night, is: what in the hell are the three of us going to do if something bad happens to Mustafa as it looks like what might be happening right now?"

"First of all, don't worry about Mustafa. He is in good hands. No Adrephine. No harm will come to him." Nicola said dryly to Lindsay's raised eyebrow.

"Well then, what's going on? He's got this completely crazy idea about using his virus on the 8 million people in the City of New York, as I am sure you know. It's never going to work. I'm sure he'll get caught. And if he gets caught, Lindsay and Nicola and Dr. Maier have no source of income. That's why I mentioned the Adrephine. I thought you might have figured out the New York situation for yourself and taken matters into your own hands."

"If I had chosen to use Adrephine on Mustafa. He'd have died, leaving you and me and – as you say – Herr Doktor Maier without any source of income."

"True. But I thought that Mustafa dead would be better than Nicola in jail."

"True. It would be. But you were right when you thought I might have figured out the New York thing for myself. I did. And, so did Dr. Maier, who is just about apoplectic over the situation."

"He is? What's he going to do?"

"I told him to start making virus……in quantities small enough not to arouse the suspicion of the authorities, especially the United States Army, which is a key player, apparently, in the virus game. But to start making the virus, so that Mustafa can see some progress. When I get back to Munich I will get Maier to make several million gallons of something – even if it's fizzy water - just to keep Mustafa content.

"Lindsay, I told Maier that I was coming to London to talk to you about both him and me. I believe he will cooperate.

"Now let me ask you, what do we all need to do to keep Mustafa's money flowing to the three of us? What requirements of yours do we need to meet?"

"Well." Lindsay said looking at the ceiling. "Let me think." Pause, then. "One thing, obviously, is that Mustafa must not send me an order to cease payments to either you or Dr. Maier. The only other thing I can think of is his death. The news of his death would reach the Hiltons, and everything would come to a halt and be handed over to their solicitors."

"Ok, death or cease payments. Completely understandable.

"Lindsay, I know that this sounds like 'ego' talking; but leave Mustafa and Dr. Maier to me. Mustafa, we all need hale and hearty – but not too inquisitive. But I think we also need Maier. This Calypso Virus he has developed I think has enormous potential – potential for money. I am thinking he can safely continue making smallish does of it that can probably be sold for enormous sums of money.

"Lindsay, there may be good money in the Calypso Virus, and I will be happy to tell our friend, Dr. Maier that we need to split the profit three ways instead of two."

"I like the way you think, Nicola. But let me tell you something. At the Hiltons I run about $130 million of Mustafa's money. On my own, I run about 4 times that amount. I can't send that money to Lindsay Grace; but I can send it to anyone else, including Dr. Nicola Angelini. Do I make myself clear, Dr. Angelini?"

"Are you suggesting a partnership, Lindsay?"

"I am, Nicola. I can't do it alone." There was a considerable pause while both Lindsay and Nicola stared down into their coffee cups.

"Ok. Well, give me some time with Dr. Maier to see if we can't bring some more money to the table, ok?

"And, don't worry, I'll keep you informed from now on, every step of the way."

"I was thinking the same thing. I have something for you." Lindsay said pulling a small cellphone out of her purse.

"What's this?"

"It's a special phone. A Lindsay-phone you might say. There is only one number programmed into it – my number. My special number."

"And." She said pulling another identical phone from her purse. "This is my Nicola-phone. It's the phone I will use to call you on your special phone."

"What's this all about?" Nicola asked.

"It is a phone – that if used correctly – eliminates being overheard by any government agency like the NSA in the U.S. So, we both must use it completely correctly."

"Why? Is the NSA going to listen to us?"

"I suspect they are listening to Mustafa. And if not, they will be soon. He can be such a fool. He should never have gone to Mauritius. I told him not to. Sooner or later the Americans will focus on the foreigners present on the island right before the ship was poisoned. They will find one Mustafa al-Khalid. I am sure you know what happened to his fiancée years ago. Well, U.S. intelligence knows too. So, I think it is only a matter of time before they add two and two and get four and then start looking very closely at Mustafa. And, once they start looking at Mustafa, I think it's only a matter of time until they start looking at his friend and former roommate. So, yes, that's why I think the NSA will be listening."

"Ok. So, how do we avoid all this?"

"Nicola, it takes agencies like NSA 90 seconds to get a positive ID on the numbers they listen to. So, we need to keep our communications well under 90 seconds. That goes for texts too. No more than 400 characters. OK?"

"Sure, I can do that."

"And remember, don't try any other calls. Just to Lindsay. Got that?"

"Got it."

"Ok, now you know how to reach me."

Just then one of the hotel staff came into the bar to announce that Bob, the driver, was there to take Nicola back to the airport. Nicola stood up, looking down at Lindsay.

"Weren't there some papers I was supposed to sign?"

"Oh, yes, these." Lindsay said producing some official looking papers from her slim leather briefcase. "You don't have to read them."

"Don't you think I should?"

"Normally yes; but I've read them. You're covered. Just sign."

Nicola signed the papers as Lindsay looked at him and finally said: "Would you mind it terribly if I called you Nick? You just seem so much of a Nick to me."

"I would be happy for you to call me Nick." Pause and stare. "What can I call you?"

"Well, I don't really know. I've never heard a nickname – pardon the expression – for Lindsay. But, if you think of one, sure."

CHAPTER 21

NORTH KOREA

When Nicola got off the fight back to Munich from London and turned his phone back on, there was a voicemail from Dr. Maier. The voicemail said Maier had good news for Nicola and asked for a meeting.

"Since we both like to be out in the early afternoon, why don't we meet at the *Seehaus*. It's actually in the English Garden. They have both indoor and outdoor tables, so we'll be fine whatever the weather. So, then, Dr. Maier: 2pm at the *Seehaus*. If there's any problem, call me. If not, I'll see you there tomorrow."

❋ ❋ ❋ ❋ ❋

"Dr. Angelini, I think I have good news." Dr Maier said standing up formally as Nicola approached his table at the *Seehaus*. So much for the greeting and exchange of small talk, Nicola thought. Right to business. And using the German pronunciation of Angelini again!

"I am not certain you know the details of how we infected the American warship." Dr. Maier began. "Of course, my colleagues and I developed the Calypso Virus right here in our laboratories on the Nymphenburgerstrasse. But we had no idea of how to infect the American warship with it.

"Dr. Maier, I'm not sure I want to know how you infected the

American ship. As I'm sure Mustafa has told you, I am not involved in this matter."

"Yes, he told me. But you are his closest friend and confidant. You don't need to be involved, but I want to make sure you know what we're doing in case you need to advise our friend, Mustafa.

"You see, Dr. Angelini, over the years, we have had occasional contact with the Navy of North Korea. The North Koreans have no sympathy for the Americans. When we told them what help we wanted from them, they were only too willing to help us. Help us – that is – for a very substantial sum of money.

"So their experts from the North Korean Navy came to work with us. We taught them two critical properties of our virus: first, it is water soluble; second, it is impervious to heat. It can withstand being boiled.

"The Korean naval experts believed that the virus could be introduced into warships through the water intakes on the bottoms of their hulls where they pump in seawater to desalinate. Once desalinated it is useable for drinking, food preparation, and bathing. But since our virus is impervious to heat, it is still in the water when the sailors drink it."

"But how do they get it into the water intake under the boat?"

"Yes, well it turns out the North Koreans have done extensive research and development with UUVs and UAVs. That would be Unmanned Undersea Vehicles and Unmanned Airborne Vehicles." Dr. Maier said rather pompously.

"Drones?" Nicola said.

"So to speak." Dr. Maier said again pompously.

"So, let me get this straight. The North Korean drones searched the bottom of the American ship till they found the water intake. Then they stuck the virus on the intake, so that the next time the ship opened it, they would suck in the virus along with the seawater. Is that about right?"

"Yes, the virus is in a nylon bag. Nylon so that the water can pass right through – all the while carrying the virus with it. The nylon bag is affixed to the water intake with simple adhesives."

"So then what happens? The virus gets into the water. The sailors drink it. They all go crazy. And they all kill each other?"

"Yes, but not like that. It doesn't happen gradually as each different sailor drinks a glass of water. It happens all at once! And that is one of the great geniuses of my virus!" The Herr Doktor blurted out with obvious pride. First time Nicola had heard the good Doktor refer to Calypso as "my" virus.

"The virus is totally dormant. Totally dormant!" Dr. Maier said poking a finger in Nicola's face. "Until." Big pause. "Until it is activated."

"And, just how is it activated?" Nicola asked.

"With an electronic signal!" Dr. Maier said with a satisfied smug on his face.

"Come again." Nicola said. "An electronic signal?"

"You recall I told you the North Koreans had expertise in both UUVs and UAVs? Well it was one of their UAVs that they sent out after the American warship. At the appropriate time, when the American ship was about 150 miles from any landfall - so that they could not possibly be rescued - they signaled the drone to send the virus activation signal to the American ship. It was then, and only then, that the violence and the murdering began."

"That's quite a story, Dr. Maier. Congratulations on your brilliant invention of the Calypso Virus, and of your equally ingenious deployment of it."

"I am very honored that you would say that, sir."

After a few minutes, allowing Dr. Maier to revel in his own brilliance, Nicola said: "Dr. Maier, when you suggested our meeting today, you had some good news. All you have told me this afternoon is good news, indeed; but is there anything else?"

"Yes, the good news is that our North Korean friends have asked us to prepare some doses of the virus. I have told Mustafa that we should cooperate with them as we prepare the much larger quantities that Mustafa wants."

"I'll be damned. The North Koreans? What do you suppose they need the Calypso virus for?"

"The United States Navy's Seventh Fleet." Dr. Maier said quietly.

CHAPTER 22

THE DOLPHIN GIRL

"Admiral?" Master Chief Petty Officer Rodrigo Montoya said into the intercom.

"Yes, Chief." Admiral Molly McNamara, the Chief of Naval Operations, responded.

"There is a Commander Sherill Kebrich on the phone from the San Diego base. Insists on talking to you personally. Says you know her."

"Ah, Sheri Kebrich!" Molly said. "I do know her. What line is she on?"

"Four, Ma'am."

"Thanks, Chief."

"Are your dolphins busy protecting my ships, Commander?"

Sheri laughed. "They are, indeed, Admiral!" They both laughed.

"I'll bet I know why you're calling."

"I'm sure you do, Admiral."

"It's about my request for a dolphin expert to be detailed to my office, isn't it? Are you coming yourself, Sheri?"

"No. Something much better."

"Oh?"

"I don't quite know how put this. I don't mean to denigrate any of my staff. But….well. With a bit of natural talent and a bucket full of fish, anyone can get a dolphin to do a lot of useful and important things. That said, I am sending you a young lieutenant named Perri DeJarnette who is definitely not your average dolphin trainer."

"Oh? How is this Lieutenant DeJarnette so special?"

"Again, I don't know quite how to say this……. Admiral. Perri can actually communicate directly with the dolphins."

"What exactly does that mean, Sheri?"

"It's very hard to explain, Admiral. Four things come to mind. First, they know when she's coming no matter what time of day. They start doing the exercises she's taught them long before she gets to the pool. Second, she can get them to do specific exercises when she's in her office – nowhere near the pool nor any dolphins. And, third, as you might imagine, Admiral, dolphins, like many mammals or other animals, gradually get to know and form relationships with humans who deal with them over the course of time. The more they see of you, the friendlier they get.

"Well when our team goes out on the open ocean for training missions, wild dolphins come right up to her. They let her ride them. And they do any exercises she asks of them. I emphasize that these are totally wild dolphins – that have never seen her before nor has she ever seen them.

"Fourth, and finally. In terms of dolphin training, Perri can do in one day what it takes my other people a month to do. And after she teaches them an exercise, they will only do it for her for – like – a month – before they will do the same exercise for any other trainer. I don't know what more I can say except that Lieutenant DeJarnette is so special.

"Admiral, whatever you need her for, when she's done, I'd like to ask your help getting a study done to find out just how she does what she does. Is she clairvoyant, or what? We – the Navy – need to learn how to do what she does – for national security reasons. I mean, if Perri can do all this, who else can? And how do we protect ourselves?

"So, I don't know why you need a dolphin expert, Admiral. It's none of my business. But I'm guessing it's very, very important. That's why I want to send you my best. And that's why I wanted to call to let you know just how good she is."

"Gosh, Sheri. I'm so glad and grateful you called. Yes, the matter is very important and highly classified. Please tell Lieutenant

DeJarnette to report to my office personally. After what you've said about her, I definitely want to meet her.

"And, by the way, when we're finished here I will definitely arrange for the studies of Perri's talents that you want."

"Thank you so much, Admiral."

"Thank YOU, Commander."

CHAPTER 23

FORT DETRICK

"So this is it, huh?" Agent Michael Cornell said lifting up a corner of the nylon bag in the box in front of him, like it was a piece of human excrement. "This is how they got the virus on board?"

"Well, it was stuck on the water intake." Lieutenant Brea Sisk said. "Do you want us to start the debriefing?"

"We need Swift and one more character whom were adding to the team."

"You mean the Admiral's dolphin expert got here already?"

"What? What dolphin expert? I was referring to a Dr. John Harmon, a virus expert from Ft. Detrick."

"Oh!" Brea said. "I thought you were referring to Admiral McNamara's dolphin expert who's also going to be joining us."

"Dolphin expert? Why does the Admiral think we need a dolphin expert?"

"Because this bag of virus had to have gotten stuck to the bottom of our ship somehow. Some one or some thing must have put it there. Probably a diver. The best way to keep divers away from our ships is to train dolphins to stop them."

"Oh." Michael said. "As usual, the Admiral is a couple steps ahead of us."

"That's why she is who she is and is in the position that she's in." Brea said with a smile.

"I guess so." Michael said.

Just then Jim Griffin appeared at the door of the Command Center with Tim Swift and a tall thin gentleman with grey hair combed back.

"This, ladies and gentlemen." Griff said gesturing to all those in the room. "Is Dr. John Harmon. Dr. Harmon is a Colonel in the Army stationed in the labs at Ft. Detrick and is also a professor at the Johns Hopkins School of Medicine."

"Welcome, Dr. Harmon." Michael said on behalf of everyone.

"Ok, Brea. Why don't you and Thea take it away and tell us what you learned out in the Indian Ocean? That work for you, Tim?" Michael said addressing Tim Swift.

"Fine."

So, Brea began with the search of every inch of the ship. "Other than the fact that it was pretty evident that a whole lot of people were murdered, there was nothing out of place. No evidence at all as to what caused the mayhem. No unusual objects or containers or instruments of any kind. Thea?"

"So we got some of the divers from the base to inspect the hull. And that's where we found this." Thea said moving to the box with the nylon bag and picking up the bag for the others to see. There was a soft but audible gasp when Thea picked up the nylon bag.

"Oh, don't worry it's completely decontaminated. Dr. Harmon's people took care of that."

"Yes, that's right. It came here in a quarantined container, but after examining it we decontaminated it. We put it through an ozonator." Dr. Harmon said.

"An ozonator?" Michael asked.

"Yes, with an ozonator we put a powerful electrical charge on it. Nothing can live through such a trauma. So, whatever traces of virus there were on the bag – and I think we found a few – the virus is now completely dead and inert."

"This is just a semi-porous nylon bag." Thea went on. It is semi-porus so that seawater can move through it. The porosity also allows substances in the bag to move with the seawater. So, what we have here is a means by which foreign substances – the size of viruses, that is - can be introduced into the drinking water of a ship.

"So, what I think we are looking at in the case of the *Little Rock*, is that someone introduced a virus into the drinking water of the ship infecting all of the crew. Then, somehow, some time much later, they activated the virus. The virus was programmed to produce rage and hysteria. So, all of a sudden, there were 36 U.S. Navy personnel running around the ship trying to kill each other. And, as you know, they succeeded. All of them."

"Is that ok, Michael?" Thea said.

"Perfect." Michael responded.

"So, my friends, as you can see. We have just witnessed terrorism being taken to a new level. This is not a suicide bomber killing himself and a couple dozen people in a crowded movie theater. This is some very sophisticated work.

"Why don't we discuss the amazing visitors to Mauritius just before our ship was poisoned. Tim, you want to lead this with what your people found out in Mauritius. Then Jake and Brea can tell us what we've learned about these people subsequently. Ok?"

"First, we owe a debt to the Customs & Immigration people on Mauritius." Tim began. "They became suspicious of a couple of their visitors and they followed up by checking them out.

"Two days before the *Little Rock* got to Mauritius, the island had five unusual visitors. They had a Turk with a German passport. They had two Germans in middle class business clothes and they had two Asians. The Asians' passports said they were South Korean. The passports were false. There were no Korean passports issued in the names of the two men. Jake?" Tim said gesturing to Jekielek.

Jake stood and told the room that the FBI had subsequently found out more information about four of the visitors, the Koreans and the Germans. He said that both of the Koreans were commanders in the North Korean Navy, the Korean Peoples' Navy, or KPN. One was stationed at the North Korean consulate in Berlin. The other was from Pyongyang but was an expert in shipbuilding. The two Germans worked for a notorious organization well known to the FBI. They worked for a scientific think-tank that rented themselves out to make instruments and destructive devices for terrorists. Jake looked out into a sea of shocked faces and then turned the floor over to Brea.

Brea told the group what Admiral McNamara had told her about the Turkish professor who taught at the University in Munich.

When people began to collect their composure, Michael stepped up and said: "With a billionaire terrorist mastermind in Munich as well as two scientists as well as a North Korean naval attaché all in Germany, guess where our next stop is? As we speak Director Slevin is at the White House getting permission for us to bring in the *Bundesnachrichtendienst*, which is the German CIA.

CHAPTER 24

LUKAS FROUMAN

"I take it you persuaded the President that we need to bring in the Germans." Michael said to FBI Director Jim Slevin. "Are we going to use our Berlin or Frankfurt office as liaison?"

"Neither, we are going to use Michael Cornell as liaison." Slevin said grinning.

"What fresh hell is this?" Michael asked.

"What do you mean 'fresh hell'? You speak German, don't you? You've been there a half a dozen times too, haven't you?"

"So, what are we going to do? Transatlantic liaison?"

"Now, listen. Here's what the President is thinking. The President wants to keep this matter as close as possible. That's why your Command Center team are the only ones who know. She doesn't want Berlin or Frankfurt to know.

"So, the President wants you to go to Munich. Meet a BND counterpart. And develop a relationship in a matter of hours that will stand you both well when you return here.

"The President is placing a call to Chancellor Merkel early tomorrow morning. She will ask that one, and only one, BND officer be assigned to work with you and that the entire matter be kept in strictest confidence.

"So, that's the story, Michael my boy. Does it really sound like 'fresh hell'?

"No. Actually it doesn't. It actually makes a lot of sense. I have been concerned about bringing in the Germans figuring somehow the story would get all over town. But, if what the President said are the ground rules, then that's great. It will be perfect just to work with one person. I just hope this German guy is very cool."

"I'm sure he'll be just as cool as you are, Mikey Boy." Slevin said knowing Michael hated being called that. "Go, pack your bags for Munich."

"Oh, one more thing before you go. I am sure your new buddies at the BND will put all of our friends in Munich and Berlin under surveillance, both electronic and physical. But, we need to start electronic surveillance at our end, too. So, while you're gone, I'm going out to the National Security Agency. Gary Gill is going to point me to the right person and get the President's ok to bring them in. That means, when you get back, you'll have another member to your team. You ok with all this?"

"Why don't you go to Munich and I'll go to the NSA?" Michael asked with mock seriousness.

"Why don't you go straight to hell?" Slevin said back with a grin, adding: "And safe travels!"

❅ ❅ ❅ ❅ ❅

The next evening at 5:30pm, Michael took off on United 106 from Dulles to Munich. Both United and Lufthansa flew direct from Dulles to Munich. If Michael had been paying for his own ticket, he would have flown Lufthansa. He liked their service. But since the U.S. taxpayers were paying, he felt guilty about flying a foreign flag when there was an American one just as readily available. So he flew United.

Same with his hotel in Munich. He booked himself into the Sheraton München Westpark Hotel. He would have much preferred a small, elegant German hotel; but again the American taxpayers were footing the bill, so he stayed at an American hotel. He also had a guilty conscience about cost. So the Sheraton's rates were very reasonable. The only problem was that it wasn't conveniently downtown. It was a good cab ride to the southwest. The Sheraton did, however, offer airport pick-up by limo. The airport was a good distance northeast of the city, so Michael allowed himself the perk of the limo pick-up.

Michael's first stop in Munich was to check in with the U.S. Consulate. He needed to check in with the head of security, who was the both the most senior and the only U.S. law enforcement officer in Munich. His name was Michael McGee and he was with the Diplomatic Security Service. He was in charge of security at the consulate.

McGee came down to meet Michael as he was going through the consulate's elaborate security.

"Agent Cornell?" He said.

"I prefer Mike or Michael." Michael said holding out his hand.

"Me too." McGee said. "Come on in."

McGee led the way to his office on the second floor. "Well, in view of the secrecy surrounding your presence, I gather this will be a short meeting."

"I guess so. The President said she didn't even tell Chancellor Merkel."

"Well, this message is for you. I didn't read it." McGee said handing Michael a small piece of paper. It said: "Agent Michael Cornell will work with Agent Lukas Frouman at the BND."

"Ok, as I assumed, it looks like my next stop is the BND."

"Oh, you'll be working with the locals. They're good people. Do you know where the BND is located?"

"No. Do you?"

"Yes, it's at 30 Heilmannstrasse in the northern suburb of Pullach."

"I can get a cab to take me there?"

"Of course, but that won't be necessary. The least we can do is give you a ride out there."

"That's very kind of you."

"As I said, it's the least we can do."

❈ ❈ ❈ ❈ ❈

To say that 30 Heilmannstrasse is imposing is an understatement. It is preceded by about a mile of 2-meter grey concrete walls with concertina wire on top. Then there's a small driveway with a small sign to the right that just says *Bundesnachrichtendienst*. That's all there is on the outside.

"Agent Frouman!" Michael said extending his hand as a tall, slim 40-ish brown head of hair walked into the security area."

"Ja."

Ich bin Michael Cornell von dem FBI. Es freut mich Sie kennenzulernen.

"I didn't know we were going to do this in German. I was hoping to practice my English." Lukas Frouman said.

"Certainly works for me. Didn't know you spoke English." Michael said.

"Went to Colgate. Come, we will need to speak in a secure area."

Michael followed Lukas out of the security building, across a courtyard and into another low building.

Once ensconced in a windowless, soundproof room, Michael began the long story that started on Mauritius.

A few minutes later, Michael noticed Lukas writing furiously in a notebook. "Lukas, I'm not sure it's a good idea to have a written record of this conversation."

"I understand, Michael. I just intend to write this down and commit it to memory. Then I will destroy the pages."

"You can actually do that?" Michael asked incredulously.

"Yes. And by the way, in college everyone called me Luke. I'd prefer you call me that rather than Lukas."

"Done, Luke." Michael said with a broad grin.

About two hours later, Michael had pretty much finished up with the narrative. Luke listened attentively. But when Michael began to describe the role of the *Stiftung Erdlust*, Luke had to interrupt. "We know those bastards. But we've never been able to get anything on them." Luke went on to tell Michael what little the BND actually knew about the *Stiftung Erdlust*. After that, Michael finished his briefing and Luke suggested they take a break and get some coffee.

"Good." Said Michael. "Then we'll figure out what to do next, ok, Luke?"

"Works for me." Luke said.

⁕ ⁕ ⁕ ⁕ ⁕

"Luke, I think we have three items on our agenda: Mustafa, the *Stiftung Erdlust*, and this Commander Ri Sang Soo at the North Korean Consulate in Berlin."

"Agreed. I assume your NSA is listening to all three of them. We will also. In addition, we will set up physical surveillance on both the Foundation and Mustafa.

"As far as the Consulate is concerned, I don't know what we can do other than listen to them. If Ri comes to Munich to talk to the Foundation, we'll pick him up on our Foundation surveillance. Otherwise, shadowing him around Berlin doesn't seem like we'd learn very much. There's no Berlin connection that I've missed, is there?"

"No." Michael said. "And I agree with you about surveillance for Ri in Berlin. No point in that."

"Ok, well then, let's get to it." Luke said with a smile.

"Ok. Let's set up our phones. Why don't you call me right now?" Michael said reciting his phone number. When the phone rang, Michael put Luke's name in his caller ID. Luke did the same with Michael's phone number.

"Ok." Michael said. "Let's talk often. Whenever there's a development, no matter how small."

"Agreed." Luke said extending his hand to Michael.

CHAPTER 25

THE THIRD MAN

"You said you get in early and I guess you really do." Said Luke Frouman over his special phone to Michael. It was 6:30am in D.C.

"I actually just got here. Haven't even had a coffee yet. What's up?"

"We have a very interesting development. It looks like we have a new player in the game."

"Oh? A new player? Who?"

"A Doctor Nicola Angelini."

"Who the hell is he?"

"Well, we first noticed him coming and going at Mustafa's apartment building. We put him in the third floor apartment. Mustafa lives on five. At first, we didn't think much of it. Then, yesterday, our man who was following Dr. Maier spotted Angelini and Maier having lunch together in a restaurant in the English Garden. So, we decided to do some more checking on Dr. Angelini.

"It turns our Angelini and Mustafa were roommates at a very exclusive boarding school in Switzerland. Angelini is Swiss. His mother and father both worked at the school. Mustafa came to Munich for university. Angelini stayed in Switzerland, studied medicine, and became a doctor. But that's just the beginning. Angelini was arrested in Switzerland last year on suspicion of murdering some of his wealthy patients after they had written very large checks to him. Apparently the Swiss magistrates gave Angelini the option of leaving the country or going on trial for murder. A few weeks later he shows up in Munich at Mustafa's. And get this. Guess who paid for Angelini's apartment in Mustafa's building?"

"Don't tell me Mustafa bought his old friend an apartment!"

"That's exactly what happened."

"Wow! Mustafa buys the guy an apartment. The guy has lunch with Maier. I guess we really do have a new player in this game. I wonder what his role is, or is going to be?"

"Can't tell yet. But we now have another suspect and another surveillance in place."

"Do you have anything that you can send us on Angelini? I'd like to share your news with my team here."

"Sure. We have an unclassified file. Nothing about this case. Just the basic information on Angelini. I'll send it right away."

"Thanks very much, Luke. And, by the way, anything else happening over your way?"

"No. Mustafa is still going to the Foundation two or three days a week. Nothing new with either him or Maier or any of Maier's people."

❈ ❈ ❈ ❈ ❈

"Jim, we've got some new developments in Germany. Got time now. Or should I tell my people now and come back?"

"Give me five minutes. I'll come down to the Command Center. You can tell all of us at the same time."

❈ ❈ ❈ ❈ ❈

"So that, folks, is the news from Germany. We know who this Dr. Nicola Angelini is; but we don't know how, or if – actually- he fits into the puzzle. We have no idea why a doctor who murders his elderly patients would be having lunch with a mad scientist like Maier. Other than the fact that they're both murderers of sorts, we have no idea what they're doing together. I just have a strong feeling that it wasn't a social lunch."

CHAPTER 26

GOING ON OFFENSE

"Lieutenant (jg) Perri DeJarnett reporting as ordered, Ma'am." Perri said saluting as she came to attention in Molly's office.

"At ease, Lieutenant." Molly said standing behind her desk taking Perri's salute.

"May I say, Admiral, that I am a big fan of yours. But I never thought I'd get the opportunity to actually meet you."

"Well, I hope I don't disappoint you." Molly said smiling.

"I understand you've been briefed about what we need to do."

"Sort of. I understand that you don't really know whether the virus was stuck onto the bottom of the ship by a diver or by some kind of UUV, a drone."

"Well, I think we're all leaning towards a drone. But that's just because divers make bubbles and are relatively easy to spot. No?"

"Yes, I'm sure it's gotta be a drone." Perri said.

"Yes, but what kind of a drone can make it's way across a harbor, identify a ship by only its hull. Then find the water intake. Then affix the virus bag right there on the water intake. That's got to be a pretty sophisticated machine." Molly said.

"It sure does. If you'll pardon my saying so, Admiral, I don't think we have anything that can do that."

"I don't think so either." Molly said absently.

"Well, Lieutenant, I assume your dolphins can easily spot a diver under a ship; but do you think they can spot a drone. They could be pretty small. Not much bigger than the virus bag."

"Oh, of course they can, Admiral. Drones are like every other kind of vessel. They require a propulsion system to move them. Propulsion systems – no matter how quiet – make enough noise for a dolphin to hear them."

"Really? So, then, Lieutenant, do you think you can train your dolphins to spot a drone approaching one of our vessels and then notify the crew?"

"I can certainly do that, Admiral. But is that all you want. Is that all you want the dolphins to do? Just notify the crew?"

"What do you mean 'all I want them to do'? What else could they do?"

"Well, Admiral, I was thinking that the dolphins could remove the virus from the bottom of our ship and take it over to the ship it came from and then fix it to the water intake of the enemy vessel."

"Oh, my God! You could actually train your dolphins to do that?"

"Sure. They'd love it!"

"Really?" Molly said in astonishment.

"Yes. It would only take a couple weeks, max."

"Wow. That's amazing! Truly amazing!"

"Admiral, I've been thinking about this. Our first priority would be to get the dolphins to put the virus on the ship that it came from. They will be able to hear the drone the second it enters the water. They will know both the direction and distance to where the drones entered the water. So, if it's a ship, they will easily be able to find it and the water intake.

"Thea Alford says that you think the virus is activated by an electronic signal. So, if the dolphins put the virus on the enemy ship and the enemy ship is close enough to receive the virus activation signal, then it will be the enemy that is poisoned.

"But if the drones didn't come from a ship, or for some other reason, the dolphins can't get the virus onto a ship's water intake, then they could bring it back to our ship and give it to the appropriate crew members. I imagine that if Thea and the guys at Ft. Detrick get some decent samples of the virus that they'll be able to figure out both the wavelength and frequency of the signal that activates the virus. They should also be able to replicate the virus itself. So, then we will have the same weapons that our enemy has."

"Wow! That is a pretty amazing scenario you are describing, Lieutenant DeJarnette. Do you really think we can do all that?"

"I don't really see why not, Admiral. I'm sure my dolphins can do their part."

"Ok, Lieutenant, you said it would only take you a couple of weeks. What are you going to need to get going?"

"I'm thinking, Admiral, that I will need some of those casings that the virus comes in. The ones that stick on the water intakes. Then I will need permission to work in right in the shipyard at the San Diego Naval Base and directly with a few of the ships. Do you think that would be ok, Admiral? I can't imagine any of those ships' captains too pleased with my fooling around with their babies."

"No, I'm sure they won't. But that's my problem and I can handle it.

"The first call I will make is to your boss, Commander Kebrich. I'll tell her what you need so far and to be sure to provide anything else you might not have thought of that you will need to train the dolphins. I will also tell her to find out what I need to do to insure the cooperation of the captains of the ships docked there.

"Let me ask you something, Lieutenant. Let's say your training goes very smoothly and that in about two weeks or so we have a team of dolphins that can frustrate the enemy's attempts to poison our ships AND even to turn the tables on them and maybe poison a few of their sailors. How do we deploy our dolphins, say, to Asia or Africa or anywhere else that we think a virus threat might come from?"

"Admiral, we have tanks just for that purpose. The dolphins travel in the tanks while the ships are moving and when the ship stops, we put the dolphins in the water and let them get a little exercise. This works for anything other than exceedingly long distances. If you're thinking Asia or Africa, the best way to get them there is to fly them in their tanks. We do this all the time."

"Ok, Lieutenant. You've sold this Admiral. Get your gear together and get out to San Diego and start training your dolphins."

"Aye, aye, Ma'am." Perri said standing and saluting.

Molly stood and took her salute. "And Perri." The Admiral said uncharacteristically using her first name. "Good luck!"

CHAPTER 27

CELLPHONE B

When Nicola got back from his run in the English Garden, he checked the special cellphone that Lindsay had given him. He had been doing that more and more often. He had also thought about Lindsay more and more often. While he was running in the English Garden he was remembering how she looked in the bar of the Stafford Hotel in London. She wore business clothes both times. But she looked very good in them.

The cellphone was an issue at first. Lindsay said it was to keep in touch. Nicola took her at her word. When the phone didn't ring and no message showed up for a week Nicola decided to find out what was going on. Why wasn't she keeping in touch? So he texted her "What's going on"?

"Nothing." Came Lindsay's response.

"What have you been up to?"

"Just work. Why are you asking me these things? This phone is just for business."

"I thought it was to 'stay in touch'."

"Well, yes, I guess. But in a business sense."

"I thought it was more than that. More than just business."

"Well it could be, I guess. But not this phone. This is just for secure business."

"Well, I'd like to talk to you sometime about more than business."

"Yes, I'd like that. I'd like to talk to you too. But not with this phone. This phone will probably be watched and listened to. We don't want any official ears listening to us talk about each other."

"When am I going to get to see you again?"

"I don't know. I guess we could meet somewhere out of Munich. But let's not talk on this phone."

"Well, what then?"

"I'll send you another phone. Just for you and me. But not a business phone. One we can talk on."

"You're going to send me another telephone?" Nicola said incredulously.

"Yes. I'll do that. I'll send it regular mail. No one will be looking for that. So watch the mail. I'll get it today and post it."

""Okay, if you say so."

"Yes, I say so. This – the phone we're using now will be Cellphone A, only for business. The other one will be Cellphone B. That'll be for our personal use."

"Okay, I got that."

After a pause, Lindsay said. "I'm glad you want to talk to me. That's nice. I didn't know – at least, for sure. So, yes, I'll look forward to talking to you on our new Cellphone B.

"Great. And while you're sending me our new Cellphone B, please be thinking of where we can meet and see each other again. And, not for business this time. Ok?"

"Yes."

"Okay, I'll be watching the mail. And I'll talk to you soon."

CHAPTER 28

POTSDAM

There was a text message on Cellphone A. It said: "They're on to us. Electronic and physical surveillance. We need to meet. Out of Munich."

"Business?"

"Yes."

"Going to Berlin with Maier next Wednesday." Nicola texted back.

An hour later another text appeared from Lindsay: "Can you lose Maier in Berlin?"

Nicola responded: "Not easily. We're flying up together at 11."

After another hour, Lindsay texted back: "Can you take a train? The 7am will get you to Berlin at 11."

"Yes. Why?"

"Trust me. More later."

❖ ❖ ❖ ❖ ❖

By the following Monday, Nicola hadn't heard any more from Lindsay, so he texted her: "More later?"

"Sorry. Are you going to take the 7am train?"

"Yes, I told Maier I wanted to see the countryside. Never seen much of Germany."

"At the train station, make a big show about going to Berlin. Ask a lot of questions and buy your ticket right there."

"Then what?"

"Then get off the train in Potsdam. It's a suburb of Berlin. I'll meet you in the restaurant there. You can take a taxi to meet Maier later."

"Why all this complication?"

"You're being shadowed. Your shadow will leave you at the train station in Munich and call ahead to have another shadow pick you up in Berlin. Only you won't go to Berlin. You'll get off the train and meet me in Potsdam."

"Ok. See you in the restaurant at the Potsdam train station."

"Not exactly. No decent ones. I'll call you in 10 minutes. Don't pick up. Let it go to voicemail. I'll give you the name of the restaurant and address.

Ten minutes the phone rang. Nicola didn't answer. When the call went to voicemail he played it back. Lindsay's voice said: "Meet me at the Wartesaal. It's a restaurant at 98 Friedrich-Engels Strasse, which runs parallel to the station. It's a nice place. You'll like it."

✳ ✳ ✳ ✳ ✳

As he entered the Wartesaal restaurant, Nicola saw her across the room. She looked up and smiled.

"When you said 'Wartesaal' – waiting room – I thought it would be a grim, dirty old place like a real train station waiting room." Nicola said laughing.

"Nooo, silly. I told you it was nice and that you'd like it."

And, indeed, Nicola thought, it was nice. Very modern. Very bright. A very nice place to meet Lindsay, indeed.

"So, you said I'm being followed?"

"Yes. You and Maier and Mustafa and some North Koreans, including this Ri Sang Soo, the one you and Maier are supposed to meet today. He's the one who organized the North Korean role in the *Little Rock* attack.

"Nick, it's time you pull back and get out. You don't want to get into this any further. Something very big is going to go down."

"What do you mean 'something big is going to go down'? How can I get out of it?"

"Nick, the other North Korean Navy guy who was in on the Little Rock attack, Ryu Dae Hee, is here in Berlin. He flew in with the Fleet

Admiral who's in charge of the entire KPN. So, the fact that the head of the North Korean Navy is in Berlin means that something very big is going to happen. And, it is going to happen with our friend, Herr Doktor Maier. If you're involved, it could cost you your life, or you could spend the rest of it in a prison somewhere."

"Damn!" Nick said rocking back in his chair. "How in the hell can I get out of this meeting with Maier and the North Koreans? Maier knows I took the train this morning."

"You have been detained by the Landespolizei." Lindsay said handing Nick an official looking document.

"What the hell is this?" Nick said taking the document from Lindsay.

"It is a detention notice. It authorizes the Brandenburger Landespolizei to detain you for 24 hours."

"What?" Nick said incredulous.

"It is a little gift from a friend who teaches at the Deutsche Hochschule der Polizei. That's the German police academy. He put this document together as a favor once I found out how dangerous it would be for you to show up at the North Korean Embassy with Maier."

"What am I supposed to do with this?" Nick asked.

"Call Maier right away – before he gets to the Embassy. Tell him that the railroad police ran a check on your Swiss passport and, when they saw the little problem you had with the Swiss authorities, they then referred the matter to the police in Brandenburg who pulled you off the train in Potsdam to interrogate you."

"But, the records in Switzerland have been sealed. The railroad police couldn't have found out about me."

"Nick, that's what they told you. Maybe it's true; maybe it's not. But mistakes do happen. In any event, Dr. Maier wouldn't know anything about Swiss police records. He certainly wouldn't guess that they'd been sealed. No German would. They would never seal records like that here in Germany.

"So, call Maier. Give him the story about the Brandenburg police. Then you and I can take a ride over to the police headquarters so you'll be able to describe to Maier where you were detained. My friend at the police academy has arranged for a guided tour for both of us at police headquarters.

"Then we'll go to lunch. Then you can call Maier again and tell him you've been released and that you're taking the train back to Munich. Then you can buy a ticket and actually take the train back to Munich. Does that sound ok to you?"

"Well, you really think of everything, don't you?"

"Well, Nick, this is so important; I really hope I've thought of everything this time.

CHAPTER 29

CLARIDGE'S

Michael took the one-hour shuttle from Munich to London the morning after his meeting with Lukas Frouman. He took a cab from Heathrow to Claridge's Hotel on Brook Street in the Mayfair district of London.

Claridge's was one of the most luxurious hotels in the world. It was on Grosvenor Square, right down the street from the U.S. Embassy. It was also one of the most expensive hotels in the world. Michael would never have even considered staying there if it hadn't been for Jim Slevin, who also authorized the $600 room rate.

Michael was in London to meet with Sir Peter Donnelly, Q.C., a barrister who had represented Mustafa al-Khalid on several matters regarding his beer business. Michael had spoken to Sir Peter on the phone. He seemed to know considerably more about Mustafa than just his beer business. So, Michael told Slevin he wanted to stop off in London on the way home from Munich to talk to Sir Peter in person. Slevin told him to stay at Claridge's and to invite Sir Peter to meet with him there. "Got to show these Brits that they're not the only ones who appreciate elegance."

Michael met Sir Peter in the Main Lounge just off the reception area.

"I'm not sure how much I do know about our mutual friend, Mr. al-Khalid." Sir Peter said. "But I do know that he is involved in far more than just teaching Latin and Greek."

"Whatever you can tell me, Sir Peter, I'd be grateful." Michael said.

"Well, as you know, I have represented him on business matters, specifically as they relate to his family's beer business. As I'm sure you also know, since his family were killed in that dreadful explosion on their yacht, Mustafa has had to take over the family company, something he was utterly loathe to do.

"Mustafa couldn't sell the beer company in Turkey fast enough. Through his fiancée, who was also killed in the explosion, he was becoming more religious. As such, the beer business, being anathema in Islam, was a constant thorn in his side.

"However, he was not so religious as to get rid of the beer business completely. Rather, he just wanted to get rid of the company in Turkey. As a Muslim country, you see, the beer was a constant source of embarrassment to him in Turkey.

"But his managers persuaded him to buy a beer company in Russia and to expand into the five central Asian republics that were part of the Soviet Union. The five "stans." Kazakhstan, Kyrgyzstan, Uzbekistan, Tajikistan, and Turkmenistan.

"You see." Sir Peter said rather pompously. "The word "stan" means "land" in the Turkic languages. So, those five countries are just named after the dominant tribes there. Land of the Kazakhs. Land of the Turkmen. And so on.

"Those peoples are all relatives of the Turks. So the feeling was that a Turkish beer would be well received there. And from the money I occasionally see changing hands, I'd say they were right. Mustafa is a very, very wealthy man. That said, that's about all I really know about him, other than some hearsay."

"So far, so good, Sir Peter." Michael said. "I'd like to hear the hearsay – so to speak – if you don't mind."

"No. I don't mind. I just don't vouch for anything I am about to tell you.

"Understood." Michael said.

"When Mustafa sold his beer company in Turkey, he didn't need all of the money to buy the Russian company. And, he didn't want the money in Turkey or Germany, for that matter. So I arranged for him to meet a very unique young woman. She is young – late 20's, early

30's – but a financial wizard. She's British but she grew up in China. So she's a bit of an Asian expert too. She speaks Chinese, Japanese, and Korean. Her name is Lindsay Grace. I shall be delighted to introduce you to her.

"As you might imagine, among international money managers like Miss Grace, there is fierce competition for wealthy clients in Japan, China, and South Korea; but little or no competition at all in North Korea. I think that the concept of "wealth" seldom comes to mind when people think of North Korea.

"But, of course, there are very wealthy people in every country, no matter how poor or backward. So, Miss Grace went to work for a bank here in the City of London, Hilton & Company, which, unlike their competitors, doesn't mind dealing with North Korean clients.

"I should mention that it's not just the individual North Korean clients, it's their money too. None of the regular banks want North Korean money in any of their investment deals. However, the Hiltons don't mind. For that reason, the Hiltons seldom get invited to join mainstream investor syndicates. And so, they have developed a bit of a reputation for handling investments that none of the mainstream banks will touch. I am talking about the drug trade, the international arms trade, the managing of front companies in third world countries – that sort of thing. Perhaps not illegal, per se; but definitely on the edge of the law and certainly distasteful to traditional City bankers. Anyway, this is a business in which Miss Grace shines. Mustafa al-Khalid is one of Miss Grace's clients.

"I don't know a lot about Miss Grace's dealings with Mustafa. But she has told me that she transfers large sums of his money to a German organization in Munich. It is a so-called foundation with a very peculiar name, *"Erdlust"*. Do you speak German Agent Cornell?"

"Yes, I do."

"Then you know that it means something like "love of the earth"; but that is a very odd way of saying it."

"Yes, I know the *Stiftung Erdlust*. And, I agree that it's a very unusual name."

"Miss Grace hasn't told me precisely what this foundation is doing for Mustafa, but I gather that it is far more than just some random charity. Certainly seems so from the amount of money Miss Grace sends them each month."

"The *Stiftung Erdlust* is far from a charitable organization, Sir Peter."

"Good. Well, I'm glad you know them.

"There is one other matter you might like to know that Miss Grace has told me about Mustafa. She is now sending money regularly to a Swiss physician who apparently lives with Mustafa."

"Oh?"

"Yes. I believe Miss Grace said his name was Nicola Angelini, Dr. Nicola Angelini. She has apparently met with him and was impressed. She said that he was quite a cut above what she calls the 'low-lifes' at the foundation.

"And that, Agent Cornell, is all I can tell you because that is all I know. But, as I said, I would be delighted to introduce you to Miss Grace. Shall I arrange it?"

"Yes, Sir Peter, I'd appreciate that very much. And I thank you very much, as well, for meeting with me today."

CHAPTER 30

THE "ADMIRAL CODRINGTON"

As he walked in the front door of the Admiral Codrington pub, he noticed an attractive young woman standing at the bar in a Navy blue suit. That is what Lindsay Grace said she'd be wearing.

Sir Peter Donnelly's office had called Michael at Claridge's to tell him that Lindsay was out of town but she would be back in two days. They had left a message for her to call Michael at Claridge's. That was fine with Michael. He needed Washington to check out several things that he had learned – mostly from Sir Peter; plus just having two days to walk around London was never a burden. He had been there several times before, but he never tired of it.

When Lindsay returned to London, she called. Michael invited her to meet him at Claridge's. Lindsay demurred.

"Let's meet on neutral ground." She said with a smile in her voice.

"Ok."

"There's a good pub in Kensington called the Admiral Codrington. It's not that far from Claridge's. Do you know where Kensington is?"

"I know where the Admiral Codrington is. Mossop Street, I believe."

"I guess you've been to London before. The Admiral Codrington is where lots of your countrymen hang out."

"I'm one of my countrymen who hangs out there." Michael said as they both laughed.

"How will I recognize you?"

"Um, shoulder length brown hair, and a Navy blue suit."

"I'll find you."

And, indeed, he thought at 4 o'clock that afternoon, standing right in front of me is some shoulder length brown hair wearing a Navy blue suit. So he walked into the bar holding out his hand.

"Lindsay, I trust." Pause. "Michael Cornell." Shorter pause "How nice to meet you!"

"Likewise Agent Cornell."

"No. No. None of this 'Agent Cornell' business. It's Mike or Michael. I like both."

"Ok. I can do that. You look like a Michael to me. So, Michael it is."

"Sir Peter thinks very highly of you. He says you are both a financial genius and an Asia expert."

"That man is too kind." Lindsay responded.

"He also said that the three of us have two, maybe three, interests in common: Mustafa el-Khalid, the *Stiftung Erdlust*, and a doctor named Angelini. Sir Peter said that he introduced you to Mustafa and that he has become a client. But what about the *Stiftung Erdlust*? Why are you interested in that dubious bunch? And what about Mustafa's roommate, the doctor?"

"Well, Mustafa has me send the *Stiftung Erdlust* very sizeable amounts of money each month. So I checked them out. I have personal reasons for doing so. Dodgy bunch, indeed! It seems they do science for a fee. And they do it for all sorts of dubious people. Mother Teresa is NOT one of their clients." Lindsay said smiling. "The gang there apparently will make you a bomb, if you like. Or maybe some nerve gas. Or, maybe some poisons. Or, maybe some other drugs, if you need them. I think of them as the criminal version of 'rent-a-brain'."

"So, what are these clowns doing for Mustafa?"

"The Germans developed some kind of toxin. They have a codename for it. They call it the Calypso Virus. Strange. Naming a toxin after a Greek goddess"

"The Calypso Virus? Well I'll be damned. Calypso. Hidden. The symptoms stay hidden until activated."

"What?" Lindsay said.

"Calypso is the ancient Greek goddess of poetry. The Greeks

thought the meaning of poems was not clear. It was hidden from the reader. *Kaluptein* in Greek means 'to hide'."

"Well, I believe this Calypso Virus was intended for use against your Navy. I assume that's why we are having this conversation."

"Right on both counts. What else do you know about this Calypso virus?"

"That's all I know. Just the name they call it and that it is a toxin."

"Ok. If you can think of anything else, please let me know immediately."

"Let me ask you about our third person in common, the doctor. What about the doctor?"

"Angelini? Oh, he's just Mustafa's old roommate from boarding school. He's Swiss. He had some problems in Switzerland and so he left and came to Munich because of Mustafa. Mustafa's helping him get back on his feet."

"Is that all? I mean I know about his problems in Switzerland. And I know he's met with Mustafa and the *Stiftung Erdlust* people too. Isn't he part of Mustafa's game?"

"When you say "Mustafa's game", I assume you mean his vendetta – or whatever – against your country and your Navy? No, I don't think Angelini is involved with them. I think he just had some problems and is trying to get back on his feet."

"Ok, back to Mustafa and the *Stiftung Erdlust*. What can you tell me about them and Mustafa's vendetta – as you call it – against the United States?"

"Well, as I said, Mustafa is paying the Germans about 3 million Euros a year to develop chemical weapons to use against your country."

"They already did. The Calypso virus killed three dozen of our sailors."

"Oh, I'm sorry to hear that." Lindsay said raising both hands to her mouth. "But I guess I should have known. Anyway, there's more. I think they're planning more attacks."

"More attacks? Are you sure? How?"

"Because I continue sending them money every month. And, there's more. I'm sure you know about the North Koreans."

"The *Stiftung Erdlust* people were traveling with two North

Koreans when our ship was attacked. We think they were involved somehow. They were Navy types. Mid level officers, technician types, didn't seem like anything special. What do you know about them?"

"For about a year, I was sending them money too. Mustafa's money. Then it stopped. Now it's started again. And this time I am sending them much larger sums of money each month. That's why I think there will be more attacks."

"Oh, dear God." Michael said.

"There's more." Lindsay said. "You said that the North Koreans involved in the attack on your ship were Naval officers. Well, the North Korean who's getting Mustafa's money is the admiral in charge of the entire North Korean Navy. His name is Choi Chung Rhee, Fleet Admiral Choi Chung Rhee."

"Oh, dear God." Michael said again. "I guess it's more than just a couple of entrepreneurial North Korean sailor boys working with the Mustafa and the Germans for some extra pocket money."

"I'd guess so." Lindsay said.

"Yes, Herr Doktor Maier has been to Berlin to see the North Koreans several times. We know about the visits; but we don't know what they were all about."

"I don't either, but it's definitely more than just talking. They're both on the same big payroll."

"Oh, dear God." Michael said again, looking absently past Lindsay.

"What else can you tell me?" He said finally.

"Not much else. That's about all I know."

"Lindsay, when we started talking you said you had your own reasons for checking out the German gang. What is that all about?"

"Michael, do you remember Flight 100 four years ago?"

"Vaguely. There was a bomb on it, wasn't there?"

"Yes, exactly. It was a flight from Beirut to Rome. My sister was on that plane."

"Oh, how awful! I'm so sorry."

"Well, I think our friends at the *Stiftung Erdlust* built that bomb. I don't know for sure; but I strongly suspect they did. And I am going to find out for sure."

"Understood. Lindsay, if you like, I will ask what our people know about Flight 100, ok?

"Yes, please do. That's very kind of you." Lindsay said looking at her shoes.

"Michael, let me ask you something." She said, raising her head. "I don't think that North Korean government is directly involved."

"Why do you say that?"

"The money. Why would they need Mustafa's money? The government of North Korea doesn't need Mustafa al-Khalid's money. But, if the government is involved, it means big trouble doesn't it? I mean big international military trouble."

"Lindsay, if one nation attacks another nation's warship, that, itself, is an act of war."

"Now it's my turn to say 'dear God'." Lindsay said staring at Michael's shirt.

"What did you want to ask me a minute ago, Lindsay?"

Getting her composure back, Lindsay said: "Michael, I am going to Pyongyang next week. I have many clients there. But the one person I want to see about this Mustafa money matter is one of my oldest and best friends. His name is Ryung Jun Kee. He is the Chief of Staff to the North Korean Ministry of Defense. His father is the Minister of Defense.

"Peter and I grew up together. All of his western friends call him Peter, Peter Kee. He and I went to the International School together in Beijing when our father's were both in their respective foreign services and both stationed in China. Then Peter returned home with his family. Then my father was transferred to Pyongyang and Peter and I hung out together for four more years. Peter showed me everything there is to see in North Korea. Nothing romantic here, just friends; but very good friends.

"I want to find out if this is the North Korean government that you are dealing with."

"Lindsay, I certainly wouldn't discuss this matter with any other human being, much less an officer of the North Korean Government."

"Michael, I am definitely not going to mention the attack on your ship. I won't even have to mention your country. I just want to see if

Peter knows about the payments I've been making to Admiral Rhee. If he does, then their government is involved. If not, then I guess we have to think again. In either event, I will let you know immediately."

"Ok, Lindsay, I trust you. That's a deal."

"And let me ask you, can we keep in touch? Would you mind going to the U.S. Embassy occasionally to take a secure call, when I need to talk to you?"

"I have a much better idea." Lindsay said reaching into her purse, pulling out a small cellphone and handing it across the table. "Here." She said.

"What's this?" Michael said looking closely at it.

"It's a very special cellphone. You see I have my own science geeks so I don't have to rely on the Germans. This phone can only make calls to one number – my number – she said holding up another identical phone. Also, it can only receive calls from one number – mine – she said waving the other phone. If we keep the voice transmissions to under 90 seconds and the texts to under 400 characters, even the geniuses at your National Security Agency can't pick us up."

"Wow! Sir Peter is certainly right. You are definitely a very special lady."

Blushing a bit, Lindsay said: "Shall we use these, then?" Gesturing to the two phones.

"Certainly. That would be perfect. I'll call you when I need you. And, please call me whenever you learn anything about any of our friends that you think I should know."

"That I will do, Agent Cornell." Lindsay said standing up and smiling.

"Great!" Michael said. "And I can't tell you how nice it's been to meet you."

CHAPTER 31

NASA MEMORANDUM

United States of America

The National Security Agency

MEMORANDUM

TO: Gary Gill

           National Security Advisor

           The White House

FROM: Alison Murphy

           Associate Director – Directorate F6

           Special Collection Service

           NSA

DATE: 1 May 2017

RE: LRV

Mr. Gill,

We have acquired some information relative to the LRV and the North Korean Navy that we feel needs to be brought to the President's attention immediately.

1. As you know, the terrorist, Mustafa al-Khalid, engaged the scientists at the *Stiftung Erdlust* in Munich to develop for him a virus to infect personnel on U.S. Naval warships. In addition, because the Germans and al-Khalid were unfamiliar with naval vessels, they engaged agents of the North Korean Navy to design a system to introduce the virus into ships' water intakes. The result of this collaboration, as you know, was the infection of the crew of the *USS Little Rock*. The virus, which they produced, is called the "Calypso Virus" by al-Khalid, presumably because its symptoms are hidden, as the name Calypso implies.

2. It was al-Khalid's intent just to test the virus on U.S. Naval personnel. His real, eventual target was the New York City water system, with its 8 million+ daily users. In short, this terrorist wants to kill more than 8 million Americans.

3. Apparently the scientists at the *Stiftung Erdlust* tried to dissuade al-Khalid. They reasoned that it would take massive quantities of the virus to infect the NYC water system, far more than they could reasonably either produce or transport. Furthermore, a key enzyme in the growth of the virus is only produced in one laboratory in the world - at Ft. Detrick by the U.S. Army. (The Germans had obtained the small quantities of the enzyme they needed for the Little Rock through 3rd parties.)

4. At this point, the North Koreans apparently contacted the *Stiftung Erdlust* scientists about producing some of the virus for them. The *Stiftung Erdlust* people readily agreed. Apparently, al-Khalid had begun to suffer some seizures and was losing some of his faculties. So, the Stiftung Erdlust people were able to convince al-Khalid that the virus they are manufacturing for the North Koreans is actually the virus that they will use

to attack New York City. In this way, the sizeable amounts of money that al-Khalid has been paying the Germans each month would continue.

5. The Fleet Admiral commanding the Korean Peoples' Navy (KPN), has recently visited their embassy in Berlin and met with Dr. Horst Maier, who is the CEO of the *Stiftung Erdlust*.

6. We believe the KPN and the *Stiftung Erdlust* are targeting two US warships for infection with the LRV in the next two months. Each of these vessels will be visiting foreign ports. That is where the attacks will occur.

7. The method of introducing the virus onto these ships will be the same as was used on the *Little Rock*.

8. The first is The *USS Typhoon*, a patrol ship with a crew of 5 officers and 24 enlisted men. The *Typhoon* is en route to visit Nakhodka on the Pacific coast of Russia next week to prepare for joint Arctic patrols with the Russian Navy.

9. The second is the *USS Bunker Hill*, a Ticonderoga-class guided missile cruiser with a crew of 33 officers and approximately 375 enlisted personnel, including 27 chief petty officers, which is scheduled to pay a courtesy call visit on Hong Kong next month.

CHAPTER 32

THE SECOND ATTACK

"Dear God! An act of war! And it's at the end of the memo!" Gary Gill said as he read the NSA memo from Alison Murphy. *Not Alison's fault. Just standard US Government procedure.* He thought as he picked up his red phone to call the President.

"What's so important, Gary?" The President said when she came to the phone.

"It's the North Koreans, Ma'am. They're going to attack 2 of our ships."

"Oh, dear God! Come in right now?"

❖ ❖ ❖ ❖ ❖

"Gary, how are the North Koreans going to attack our ships? And where?"

"Russia in two weeks and next month in Hong Kong. They're going to use the Calypso Virus again. Same as against the *Little Rock*."

"Oh my dear God!" The President said again moving to the window of the Oval Office. "Gary, let's get the team here as soon as possible. We've got to deal with this right away. After we talk, I'll get the Cabinet together and get them involved too."

❖ ❖ ❖ ❖ ❖

Gary summoned the principals to the Oval Office. Admiral McNamara. Swift. Cornell. Jim Slevin. And Alison Murphy.

President Daley addressed them. "You've all seen the NSA memo." She said nodding at Alison. "You know, this is an act of war. What advice can you give me?"

"Madam President." Admiral McNamara began. The North Koreans may try to attack the *Typhoon*; but I can assure you that their attack will not succeed." There was stunned silence in the room Admiral McNamara spoke."

"Tell us what you mean, Molly." The President said.

"Madam President, my colleagues, the North Koreans will attack with the Calypso Virus, just as they attacked the *Little Rock*. This means that they will use a submerged drone to search out the *Typhoon's* water intake to which they will affix a nylon bag containing Calypso Virus. As you all know, the virus is dormant until activated by an electronic signal. The North Koreans will wait about 48 hours to be sure all of the *Typhoon's* crew have ingested the virus. Then they will send an electronic signal to activate it. When they do so, they will be shocked. They will be shocked because the virus did not infect our American sailors; rather it infected them – the sailors on the North Korean ship that sent the virus.

"You see, we have been working with these attack methods ever since the *Little Rock*. We have learned that our trained dolphins can hear the undersea drones approach our ships. The dolphins can also discern where – that is, which enemy ship – the drone came from.

"Once the drone places the virus bag on our ship, it then drops away to the ocean floor. At that point our dolphins remove the bag of virus from the bottom of our ship, carry it across the harbor to the ship it came from, find that ship's water intake, and affix the virus to the intake.

"So, later on, when the North Koreans send the electronic signal to activate the virus, they will find that it has infected their own sailors, not ours. Their own people will begin murdering each other."

"That is an incredible story." The President said, reflecting the thoughts of everyone in the room. "Are you sure it will work the way you say?"

"Yes, I am. We have been working ever since the *Little Rock*. Our dolphin people in San Diego have been driving all the ship captains out there crazy with their exercises. Our dolphins patiently wait for drones to approach the ships they are protecting. They swim around while the drones affix nylon bags to the ships' water intakes. Once the drones are gone, the dolphins remove the nylon bags from they ship they're on and take them across the harbor to the ship that launched the drone. They then put the virus bags on the water intakes of those ships. They've been doing this successfully for several weeks. I have deployed our best dolphin trainer and her three best dolphins to accompany the *Typhoon* to Russia. Not only will the *Typhoon* be safe; but the North Korean ship that tried to infect her will definitely be in harm's way."

"Even if we repel the North Korean attack, Admiral, their actions still constitute an act of war."

"Yes, Madam President."

"So, what do we do?"

"Whatever you order M'am. I have over 250,000 Marines and Naval personnel as well as over 2000 aircraft and 200 ships in the Pacific Command. My cyber-forces can blind the North Korean's radar and neutralize their countermeasures. Then, with complete control of the skies, our aircraft based in Japan can attack all 33 North Korean military bases. We would also crater bomb the runways of the 16 bases where there are North Korean aircraft, so that they can't take off or land. A handful of North Korean aircraft might manage to get off the ground, but since their radar will be jammed, they should be easy prey for our air-to-air missiles.

"And as I'm sure you know, the North Korean military is heavily concentrated in ground forces most of which are poised along their border with South Korea. We can destroy those bases where their ground forces are clustered. And, that's just us in the Navy, Madam President. There are three other branches of our military that can help, too." Admiral McNamara said to faint smiles around the room.

"So, what' your telling us, Admiral, is that the *Typhoon* and her crew are safe? And that the North Korean ship that launches the attack on the *Typhoon* will suffer the same fate as the *Little Rock* – her crew will all murder each other?"

"Yes, that right, Madam President."

"So, we need to decide what more we need to do to North Korea to punish them for trying to attack us and to deter them from these kind of attacks in the future."

"I guess so." Said Admiral McNamara with all others in the room nodding.

❁ ❁ ❁ ❁ ❁

"Wow, I had no idea you had this so well under control!" Michael said to Molly as they lingered outside a while as the others left the Oval Office.

"I try to earn my pay." Molly said with a big smile.

"You know, one thing that keeps bothering me though. When I met with Lindsay Grace she expressed doubt that it is actually the North Korean government that's involved."

"What does she think is happening?"

"Well, she has been sending millions of dollars not to the North Korean government, but to the Admiral who runs the North Korean Navy. A guy named Fleet Admiral Rhee."

"I've heard of him. But I don't know much about him. What does Lindsay think?"

"As I said, she just thinks it strange that she is sending tons of money to this guy's personal bank account. Not some official bank account of the North Korean Government."

"I guess it could be so. But that's one hell of a risk the bastard is taking. Provoking the United States of America is not a smart move for any government, but it's really a dumb move for a government official working on his own. Not only could we kill him; but so could his own people. Seriously."

"I agree. See you tonight." They both looked quickly around. Seeing no one, they kissed.

❁ ❁ ❁ ❁ ❁

As Michael walked the few short blocks back from the White House to FBI Headquarters, he remembered that there was an unopened note from the forensics lab at Fort Detrick that just was just delivered as he was leaving. He thought the note might contain an answer to the question Lindsay Grace had asked him about the fate of Flight 100 that cost Lindsay's sister her life. It did.

The note was from the team leader who analyzed the wreckage of Flight 100 some 4 years ago. The Fort Detrick scientists concluded that the bomb that destroyed Flight 100 going from Rome to Beirut was manufactured by the *Stiftung Erdlust* engineers in Munich. *Just as Lindsay thought.* Michael said to himself.

He sat down looking at the message. Finally, he took out the special cellphone that Lindsay had given him and entered the following text: "Fort Detrick says the Flight 100 bomb was manufactured by the *Stiftung Erdlust.*" He pushed send.

CHAPTER **33**

CALL FROM TOKYO

It was 8pm. As Michael was getting dressed after his squash match at the Metropolitan Club, he casually glanced at the cellphone Lindsay had given him. He was shocked to see a text message from her.

"I'm in Tokyo and need to talk to you immediately. Please authorize your embassy to let me call you. I need more than 90 seconds."

He got on to the FBI operator who put him through to security at the U.S. Embassy in Tokyo where it was 9am.

"This is Special Agent Michael Cornell. Whom am I speaking to?"

"This is Agent Ronald Maziarz of the Diplomatic Security Service. What can I do for you, Agent Cornell?"

"Agent Maziarz, one of our most important informants is in Tokyo and has some very sensitive information to pass to us. She needs to call me on your secure phone. Can you arrange that?"

"Of course. No problem. How can I reach this informant?"

"I'll have her reach you. Her name is Lindsay Grace. Michael spelled the names out. What is the local phone number I can give her to contact you?"

After Maziarz gave Michael his phone number, he thanked him and rang off.

Michael immediately picked up his "Lindsay-phone" and texted her Maziarz' name and number. He then finished dressing and headed back to the office. About 90 minutes later, Lindsay's call came through.

"Michael, I am just back from Pyongyang." Lindsay began without even saying "hello". "I have critically important news. The North Korean Ministry of Defense knows absolutely nothing about Mustafa al-Khalid, nor the *Stiftung Erdlust*, nor the millions of dollars I have delivered to Fleet Admiral Rhee, nor anything about any attack on any American Naval vessel. They know nothing.

"Michael, I talked to Peter in person. I know he was telling the truth. He was genuinely shocked. I could see it on his face and the way he held his hands. He couldn't possibly have been lying to me.

"Also, Peter volunteered to check with his people at the Ministry. He called me the next day – that was yesterday – and told me that not only did no one at the Ministry of Defense know about any of this, but no one at any of the other ministries knows anything about it either. Peter thinks – especially with all of the money involved that no one knows about – that Admiral Rhee is working on his own. He's – what do you call it – a lone ranger. The North Korean government is not involved."

"You're absolutely sure, Lindsay?"

"Yes, I know Peter. I know him like I know myself. He is not faking. He knows nothing. And he is certainly not lying."

"Well, I'll be damned." Is all Michael could think of to say.

"Michael, there's more. Admiral Rhee is on his way to a port in Russia called Nakhodka. He's going to meet one of his North Korean Naval ships that's already there. Also, Peter said something about an American Naval ship being there too. He didn't know what it was all about. He just knows that an American ship is supposed to be at the same Russian port too."

"Oh, dear God. Lindsay, I can't thank you enough. What you have told me is critically important news. I've got to move on it right now. Thanks so much once again. I'll talk to you soon."

"Michael, I'll let you go. I just wanted to say thank you for your message about Flight 100 and the *Stiftung Erdlust*."

"Sure, Lindsay. Glad we could help. God bless. Talk to you soon."

CHAPTER 34

NAKHODKA

The motto of the *USS Typhoon* is "E Malacia ad Fulmina", which is usually translated "out of the calm come the thunderbolts". But that's not really a good translation. "Malacia" comes from a Greek word that really means sickness or weakness. This makes a little more sense. By Naval standards, the *Typhoon* is a very small ship. It is a patrol vessel that only weighs 750,000 lbs and has a crew of only 4 officers and 28 sailors. For that reason, smallness may be associated with weakness. Might look weak: but it's not. Hence the motto.

The *Typhoon* docked in the northern part of Nakhodka harbor, in the inlet that leads to the train station. The Typhoon's mission was to accompany Russian patrol boats in the Arctic Ocean. This was the first time that the U.S. and Russia were holding joint patrol exercises in the Arctic.

A North Korean frigate had arrived the day before the Typhoon and docked on the opposite, peninsular side, in the southern part of the harbor. North Korea maintained a consulate in Nakhodka.

Lieutenant Perri DeJarnette and two of her dolphins had been flown from their base in San Diego into Pusan, South Korea, where they were picked up by the *Typhoon*. As soon as the *Typhoon* arrived in Nakhodka, Perri got the dolphins out of their tanks and into the water. The following day the dolphins detected an undersea drone approaching the *Typhoon*. The drone had been launched from the

North Korean frigate across the harbor. The dolphins hovered around as the drone sought out the *Typhoon*'s water intake on the ship's hull. The drone found the intake, affixed a nylon bag containing Calypso Virus to it, and then dropped off to the sea floor. As soon as the drone was gone, the dolphins removed the nylon bag containing the virus from the intake, swam across the harbor to the North Korean frigate, located its water intake and affixed the virus bag to it. From the sensors she had strapped to the dolphins, Perri knew exactly what was going on. Perri reported it to the *Typhoon's* captain who reported it directly to the Pacific Command in Hawaii and Admiral McNamara at the Pentagon.

U.S. Army units stationed in South Korea had been ordered to monitor flights of North Korean naval aircraft. The U.S. also had a cruiser in the Sea of Japan between Korea and Russia that was also listening. Both units reported that a small North Korean naval aircraft – the kind used to transport VIPs - had departed Pyongyang headed for Nakhodka.

The next morning, the *Typhoon* prepared to depart at dawn. So did the North Korean frigate. At about 6:15am, the *Typhoon* cleared the harbor entrance. Admiral McNamara had placed two NCIS agents and two Korean language specialists aboard the *Typhoon*. They were monitoring all radio transmissions between the North Korean frigate and their consulate in Nakhodka.

A voice from the North Korean frigate, who identified himself as Fleet Admiral Rhee's aide, came on the air to report that the frigate was pursuing the *Typhoon*. He ominously reported that they were preparing the aerial drone that would activate the Calpyso Virus. It would be launched in approximately 25 minutes when the *Typhoon* had crossed out of Russian territorial waters.

When the 25 minutes had passed Admiral Rhee's aide came back on the air to report that the Admiral had personally launched the drone. In five minutes he would signal the drone to send the signal activating the Calypso Virus, which they clearly believed was on the *Typhoon*.

Five minutes later the Admiral's aide was back on the air reporting that the Admiral had signaled the drone to activate the virus that they assumed was on the *Typhoon*. The aide pompously informed his radio audience that it would take a few minutes for the virus to take effect.

After about 10 minutes, the North Korean Consul listening to the radio transmissions back in Nakhodka licked his lips. It was taking longer than it should have.

Suddenly the radio went alive with screaming voices and the Admiral's aide yelling that the Admiral was dead. He had been murdered by the crew.

The next transmission was simply the screams of the Aide as he, too, was murdered by the crew.

CHAPTER 35

THE BOATHOUSE

The *USS Typhoon* was safe. The dolphins had done their job. They took the bag of Calypso Virus off the *Typhoon* and put it on the water intake of the North Korean frigate where it came from. Once it was clear that the crew aboard the North Korean frigate had all murdered each other, the Typhoon's captain notified the Pacific Command and Admiral McNamara in the Pentagon, as he had been instructed.

The Pacific Command notified a startled Russian Navy commander in Nakhodka that the North Korean frigate had become disabled and its crew incapacitated. The frigate was pursued then and boarded by the Russian Navy. It was returned to Nakhodka and would presumably be returned to the North Korean government some day after much explanation.

The White House had acted on the information Michael received from Lindsay Grace: the North Korean Government was not responsible; rather it was one man, the rogue Fleet Admiral who ran the North Korean Navy, who was to blame. That Admiral was on the North Korean frigate that was infected with the Calypso Virus. He was murdered by the ship's crew. So, the game was over.

When Admiral McNamara got the news, she texted Michael that Admiral Rhee was dead. Michael took out the special cellphone that Lindsay Grace had given him and texted: "Rhee is dead."

The following day, just as Michael was leaving Washington for the weekend, he got a call from Gary Gill at the White House. Gary told him that Secretary of State Jim Dickman had told the President that the State Department had received a curious informal message from the North Korean Government thanking the United States for the way it handled the "Fleet Admiral Rhee affair".

Gary finished by saying that the North Korean Government was pleased the way things turned out, and so was the United States Government.

So, Special Agent Michael Cornell was in a very good mood as he entered The Boathouse restaurant in Baltimore's Inner Harbor. As soon as he saw Admiral Molly McNamara – even though she was in civilian clothes - he kissed her for a little bit longer than he should have in a public place. But she just laughed, as did Michael. She was a happy Admiral now.

"What a week!" Molly said gratefully accepting a glass of red wine from the server and taking a long healthy drink out of it.

"It's not quite over yet." Michael said. "I have a little more news for you."

"Oh?"

"Yes, you remember the German bastards who manufactured the virus?"

"Yeah, the *Stiftung Erdlust* or something like that, wasn't it?"

"Yep, those are the guys. Or, I should say 'those were the guys'."

"Were?" Molly said surprised.

"Yep. When the *Typhoon* thing started to go down in the Pacific we notified the BND in Munich who raided the *Stiftung Erdlust* offices. We wanted to close the loop on this whole bloody affair by ending their careers as well, even if somewhat more gently than we ended Admiral Rhee's career. Well, when the BND got there, they found them all dead. Dr. Maier and his whole gang. All dead. The BND thinks poison."

"Really!" Molly said in disbelief.

"Yes, and there's even more. The BND knew that our friend Mustafa al-Khalid had moved into an assisted living facility in Munich. So, they paid him a visit. But when they went to question him, they found he'd turned into a vegetable. They found him in a wheel chair just staring into space. Didn't respond to questions. Didn't even respond to his own name."

"Wow, that's quite an ending to our *Little Rock* affair, isn't it. Everybody involved in infecting our sailors on the *Little Rock* with the Calypso Virus are now either dead themselves or, as in Mustafa's case, might as well be."

"Yes, indeed they are." Michael said. "And there's one more little piece to our story. You remember that doctor friend of Mustafa's, Dr. Angelini?"

"Sort of." Molly said.

"Well, the BND went to pay a call on him too. But, no Angelini. Nowhere. Gone. Totally disappeared. And, when they checked, the BND found out that he had even sold his apartment. The one in Mustafa's building. He'd sold it for cash."

"Well, that's certainly strange." Then, after a brief silence, Molly said: "Those *Stiftung Erdlust* bastards are the ones that built the bomb that killed Lindsay's sister too, aren't they? I'll bet she's not shedding any tears that they're gone."

That was something Michael hadn't thought of till then. "Yeah, I'll bet you're right." He said absently.

As Molly began to look over the menu, Michael looked out past her into Baltimore Harbor. He was thinking that he hadn't heard from Lindsay Grace since her call from the Embassy in Tokyo.

Strange. He thought. *He texts Lindsay that Admiral Rhee is dead. Next thing we get a thank-you note from the North Korean government.*

Even stranger, he texts Lindsay that the Stiftung Erdlust gang are responsible for her sister's death. Next thing, they're all dead. Poisoned.

And strangest of all, Mustafa al-Khalid, the man with the millions, is suddenly an incoherent vegetable. His money is gone. And his sidekick, Nicola Angelini, the dangerous Swiss drug doctor, is nowhere to be found.

All very strange indeed.

CHAPTER 36

ST. MAARTENS

St. Maartens is about 1700 miles from The Boathouse Restaurant in Baltimore Harbor where Special Agent Michael Cornell and the Chief of Naval Operations, Admiral Molly McNamara, were having a quiet dinner.

St. Maartens is, actually, the casual name that many Americans use to refer to one of the Leeward Islands in the Caribbean Sea that is the home to two separate countries: Sint Maarten, which is Dutch-speaking, and, Saint-Martin, which is French.

Lindsay Grace was lying on the beach in Saint-Martin. She had fallen asleep reading a catalogue of new homes for sale on Saint-Martin. She was jostled gently awake by the man lying next to her.

"Where shall we go for dinner tonight, my love?" He said.

"Oh, I don't know, Dr. Angelini." Lindsay said with a yawn that turned into a big smile. "Why don't you make the decision for us?"

19860691R00104

Made in the USA
Middletown, DE
07 December 2018